One More Day to Go

David Snook

Pen Press

Copyright © David Snook 2009

All rights reserved

No part of this publication may be reproduced,
stored in a retrieval system, or transmitted
in any form or by any means, without
the prior permission in writing of the publisher,
nor be otherwise circulated in any form of binding or cover
other than that in which it is published and without a similar
condition including this condition being imposed on the
subsequent purchaser.

First published in Great Britain by
Pen Press Publishers Ltd
25 Eastern Place
Brighton
BN2 1GJ

ISBN 978-1-906710-66-8

Printed and bound in the UK

A catalogue record of this book is available from
the British Library

For me, life is the most precious commodity in the universe. Therefore I dedicate this book to the memory of my friend

David Cooper
(Cooperman)

*A sometimes cantankerous, sometimes stubborn, but always loveable Liverpudlian, who bridged the cultural differences between Cockney and Scouse,
and who fought so very, very hard for just one more day.*

About The Author

Like Tom Hall in our story, the author was the seventh child born into a working class family just prior to the second world war. Considered to be reasonably bright by most of his teachers and contemporaries, he was hampered by an inbuilt destruct button which was activated whenever disciplined or forced to concentrate on his studies. A result of which meant that by today's standards he would probably be considered to be poorly educated. This did not bode well for his later ambitions to enter into the literary world. However the stubborn streak that impeded the author's early life, was in the end to prove invaluable when venturing into the real world to try and earn a living.

After a reasonably successful career in the construction industry, as well as spending a considerable amount of his leisure time either helping to raise funds for various good causes, or working with young people, he is now enjoying a comfortable retirement. Concentrating at last on all the things that as a child was too stupid to appreciate.

David Snook has one previous title published by Pen Press, *Tosser or Tearaway*.

One more day is all I ask
That I may say to you
All the things I should have said
But just assumed you knew

If not a day, an hour perhaps
To think about the past
To lay there in your arms again
Protected from life's blast

An hour to recall the times
That made our lives worthwhile
The silly and forgotten things
That always raised a smile

A minute would be wonderful
In order to placate
The conscience of a miscreant
Before it is too late

A second longer will suffice
In which to pledge to you
This ephemeral moment
To prove my love is true

A lifetime I have wasted
Living in a reverie

When all the time before my eyes
You were there in front of me

The sands of time relentlessly
Continue on their path
Across the plain of life
Regardless of the aftermath

Life is brief and can be cruel
While memories fade away
But for this I'd have no need
To beg for one more day

D.W.Snook
08.08.08

1

December 27th 2038
Eastbourne, England

Tom lay there in that lovely half-awake, half-asleep state. The bed felt nice and warm as he drifted in and out of consciousness; he wished he could lie there forever, but he knew this would not be possible. Some bugger would come and disturb him no doubt.

No sooner had this thought crossed his mind than there was a gentle knock on the door and in breezed Mary.

"Morning Tom, how are we today?"

We were bloody fine until you walked in, he said to himself, but remained motionless.

"It's another lovely day, Tom, especially for this time of the year. Are you going to join us for breakfast, or do you want t'have it in your room?"

It's a long time since I have had it in my room as well, thought Tom, but then he wasn't thinking about breakfast.

Mary moved over to the window to draw the curtains. Tom lay there feigning sleep; he did, however, move his head slightly to one side allowing his eyelids to part just enough so that he could observe the proceedings.

Mary must have been all of 19 or maybe 20 years of age, 5ft 6in tall with auburn hair. She had the most slender thighs, supporting what Tom guessed was the best looking arse in the care home. Her waist was slim and fragile, and when she moved those hips it sent so many distant memories flooding through Tom's mind that he nearly forgot he was supposed to be asleep.

With perfectly formed breasts tucked inside the blouse of her uniform, she was the most beautiful young woman he had seen for many a long year. Not since his beloved Jenny in fact. As the curtains parted, the winter sunshine came flooding into the room. For a brief moment Mary was silhouetted in front of the window; you could clearly see the outline of her body beneath a flimsy white uniform. It was days like these that made Tom think life was still worth living. Having finished with the curtains and checked the weather outside, Mary turned her attention to Tom. Pausing at his bedside she leaned over and peered at his still half-turned head, allowing her breasts to hang perilously close to his face. As she studied him she detected a slight tremor. The crafty old bugger was awake. Nevertheless she let her breasts remain where they were for a few more seconds, a glimmer of a smile crossing her lips.

She liked Tom; he rarely complained about anything. Unlike some of the others in her care, he never overstepped the mark. His eyes, despite his age, had a warm glow, a certain sparkle that in a younger man would have made her go weak at the knees. He made her aware of her sexuality without making her feel uncomfortable, a feat that many men a quarter of his age had failed to do. Then she knew Tom liked women and felt at ease in their company.

Mary decided not to deny him his brief moment of pleasure; after all it was his birthday tomorrow. "Come on Tom, wakey, wakey; it's time to face the world."

Tom allowed himself to stir; he opened his eyes and raised his head off the pillow. "Morning Mary, you look as beautiful as ever; that young man of yours doesn't know how lucky he is."

"You old flatterer! He knows, don't you worry; I make sure of that. Now are you going to join the others for breakfast or not?"

"I think I'll have breakfast in bed today Mary, if you don't mind. It's my big day tomorrow and I want to conserve my energy."

A look of concern crossed Mary's face. "You are feeling all right, aren't you Tom? Shall I ask Miss Branigan to ring Dr Cohen?"

Tom laughed, "Don't panic, Mary, I'm fine; just feeling a little tired today. I'll stay here a moment or two longer and prepare myself for tomorrow." He didn't want Martha Branigan getting involved; in his opinion she was too full of her own importance.

As the home's administrator, Martha Branigan was in charge of ensuring that everything ran smoothly with staff and residents. Her way of doing this was to let them all know in no uncertain terms who was boss. Now in her late forties, and still unmarried. All that, however, was about to change. Recent events concerning a Dr Cohen had turned her whole life upside down. Her sympathy and understanding during his recent bereavement had paid dividends. Although he was older than her by some eight or nine years, he was quite well preserved and very fit, as he had proved to her on their recent night of passion, at the end of which he had proposed to her. The thought of becoming the wife of a doctor, of David Cohen's calibre, with all its trappings and social standing, appealed to her ego. Nobody, but nobody – especially Tom Hall – was going to spoil her plans to advance her profile.

Martha's parents had been blessed with their daughter when they were middle-aged, hence the fact that they had spoilt her at every opportunity, forever telling her she was a gift from God, after remaining childless for so many years. Therefore getting what she wanted came naturally to her.

Tom viewed the situation differently, however. If he could prevent her from getting her own way just once before he shuffled off this mortal coil, life would have been worthwhile. He hadn't forgiven her for trying to get him into a smaller room soon after she had arrived. Martha had only been in charge a couple of months, having replaced the previous administration within three weeks of Tom's arrival. He smiled as he recalled their first real conversation.

"Good morning Mr Hall, I trust you are keeping well?"

"Well enough thank you," Tom replied.

Before he could continue Martha cut him short. "I've been thinking, Thomas – you don't mind if I call you Thomas do you? – it's in keeping with my policy of making friends with all our residents.

Tom didn't care what Martha Branigan called him, but past experience had taught him that over-familiarity usually meant the person trying to be friendly wanted something.

Unabashed by Tom's obvious wariness, Martha ploughed on. "As I say, I have been thinking, and I feel you would be more comfortable if you moved in with Robert Downing. You both seem to get along very well together, and the company will be good for the pair of you. I will arrange to have your things moved tomorrow morning."

Tom's eyes narrowed. So, he had been right. He could see this woman was used to getting her own way and riding roughshod over anyone who got in her path. Well, he had spent his whole life dealing with difficult people. He cut her short. "May I point out, Miss Branigan, I have a legally binding contract with this home that allows me to stay where I am in this particular room for as long as I think fit. Furthermore, although as you put it, I get on well with Robert Downing, I have no wish to set up home with him, or anybody else for that matter. As for what may or may not be good for me, I think I am in a better position than you to decide. I may be old but I am not yet incapable of thinking for myself."

Martha Branigan face turned a deep shade of purple; nobody had ever spoken to her like that before, and it was obvious that this old bugger was no pushover. She had taken the trouble to examine the contracts of all the residents and in particular Tom Hall's, before making her approach. She had doubts as to whether he could be moved, but as all the other inmates had agreed to her suggestions regarding their welfare she saw no reason for him to object. This was the first time someone had questioned her authority and she didn't like it.

"Try not to get upset, Thomas, I am only thinking of what would be best for you."

"I'm not getting upset," replied Tom curtly, "as I have just told you, I am quite capable of making my own decisions and I have no intention of moving from this room. I will contact my solicitor in the morning and ask him to sort this matter out for me."

"Now, let's not be too hasty, Thomas," said Martha Branigan, "I am sure we can work something out. I did not realise how strongly you felt about it; we will leave things as they are until you have a change of heart."

Or until you think I'm too bloody senile to object, Tom thought. But he kept that particular thought to himself.

Two weeks later a subdued Martha Branigan entered Tom's room. "I have been in contact with the governing body of our care home and it appears your contract with them is indeed legally binding. Therefore I have decided to let the matter drop. I just thought I would let you know to put your mind at rest."

Dragging himself back to reality, Tom pondered on his forthcoming birthday. No, he certainly did not want Martha Branigan alerted to anything. Time enough when tomorrow finally arrived and she assumed her role as self-appointed director of operations. Anyway, it was no big deal these days for people to reach his age, unlike when he was a boy. He remembered how, back then he used to think anyone who reached 50 was old and decrepit.

A knock on the door disturbed Tom's thoughts; it was Pearl with his breakfast on a tray. She sat herself down opposite as he started to eat, patiently waiting for him to finish before asking him how he was.

It should have been Pearl's day off and she planned to spend it in London with Malcolm, but because it was such an important day tomorrow she had decided to look in on her favourite patient. Malcolm had an opportunity to join the Westminster Abbey choir and Pearl thought it would be nice to walk along the embankment while he was auditioning, then have lunch together by the river.

Pearl liked talking to Tom; his mind was still sharp and his memory clear. Well, she assumed it was clear, he had outlived all his contemporaries so there was no one left alive to contradict him. Chatting away to him, Pearl realised that Tom had probably lived through the reign of more kings and queens than anyone she knew. He had laughed when asked if he remembered Queen Victoria. "I'm not that bloody old," he replied. He did remember George VI, Queen Elizabeth II, Charles' brief reign up until the present King William. "You can safely bet he will be the last King I will ever see," he chuckled.

Pearl gathered together the breakfast dishes and placed them back on the tray ready to depart, but not before she had made sure Tom was wrapped up nice and warm in his chair.

If anything happened to him before tomorrow and he was unable to take part in Martha's plans, she would be for the high jump.

Just as she was about to leave, Pearl remembered an incident that had taken place earlier in the week. It had slipped her mind what with all that had been going on recently. "By the way, Tom, there was a lady making enquiries about you the other day, a Mrs Samantha Edwards. I believe she wanted to come and see you, but I think Martha suggested she wait until the New Year."

Tom looked puzzled. "Samantha Edwards? I don't think I've ever heard of her, but then my memory isn't what it used to be. We will have to wait and see if she bothers to come back."

2

Arrival

Dorothy Hall was mulling over the past year as she lay in the maternity wing of St James hospital. God, it had been an awful 12 months. Finding out she was expecting another baby so soon after losing John, she had led her husband George a dog's life. Although only 38, Dorothy had already given birth to six children, this would be her seventh. This one was definitely a mistake.

Of course her parents had warned her about marrying George in the first place. "A rum lot," her father had said. She wished now that she had listened to their advice.

When John had died at the tender age of two, George had promised her they would have no more children. George being George, however, within a year of their loss he had arrived home the worse for drink, and despite her pleas for caution, she found herself pregnant again.

Her thoughts were disturbed by the sound of church bells ringing in the distance; St Mary's was summoning the righteous to midnight mass. A sudden pain in her stomach made Dorothy wince; they were coming more frequently now, her experience told her that it would not be long now before the baby arrived. Perhaps she should ring for the nurse. Her mind drifted back to John; such a lovely boy, with the most beautiful brown eyes, all her other children had blue eyes like their father. John had been different. Dorothy liked to think he took after her side of the family, but now he was gone and she was stuck in this bloody hospital going through it all again.

She had only let go of John's hand for the briefest of moments to light a cigarette. Everyone at the time had said that the tram driver never had a chance of stopping. All Dorothy remembered was the sudden squeal of brakes followed by a dull thud; after that everything else was a blur. The people gathering around, the clang of the ambulance bell as it rushed to the scene, even the journey in the back of the ambulance on the way to the hospital she barely remembered. The only part that would stick in her mind for the rest of her life was when the doctor, accompanied by a severe looking matron, informed her John was dead. Dorothy had never touched another cigarette since.

Again she felt the pain. It was bound to be a boy. Having been messed about by the male gender for most of her life she knew it couldn't be anything else. The pain was increasing every two or three minutes, surely the little bugger was coming now? Unable to control herself any longer Dorothy let out a scream.

A severe looking midwife popped her head round the ward-room door. "It's all right, Mother, I'm here now, no need to make such a fuss." No need to make a fuss? How the fuck did she know? She wasn't the one in pain, probably never had a man in her life, let alone a baby. Dorothy let out another yell as she felt the baby's head appear. Bloody hell how it hurt; she was sure it was a boy. They fought like mad to come out and as soon as they reached puberty they spent every waking moment of their lives trying to get back in again.

When the birth was finally over, a delighted midwife exclaimed, "It's a boy, a lovely baby boy, with the most beautiful dark brown eyes. You realise it's Holy Innocents day today, Mother, don't you? He will be blessed with long life and good fortune."

Dorothy didn't know what day of the week it was, let alone Holy Innocents day. She couldn't have cared less, the pain had gone, and suddenly she felt very tired. This baby had already spoilt her Christmas, the last thing he would probably turn out to be was innocent.

The midwife produced one of her rare smiles; another man born into the world. This one seemed to have caused enough trouble even before he got here. Turning to Dorothy she said, "I had my doubts whether this baby would arrive before the New Year but he has. What are you going to call him?" Thomas, thought Dorothy as she drifted off into a deep sleep, Thomas Jonathan Hall.

And so Tom came into this world, a world that would soon be plunged into war. His would experience a childhood of air raid sirens, falling bombs and food rationing. Nearly a century later Tom's recollection of these times was sketchy. The sound of falling bombs and the wail of the sirens were to remain in his memory all his life, however. He also had vague recollections of being evacuated together with his brothers and sisters to some weird farm in Sussex, of being told how lucky he was to be there and that if he didn't behave he would be packed off back to London.

His mother must have become fed up with being told the same thing, because within the year she had carted them all back to the metropolis, preferring perhaps the city bombs to the verbal barrage of the countryside. Back home life became even more stressful. With the countless air raids and forever having to stand holding on to his mother as they queued for the weekly food ration, it was a wonder he survived at all. Plus the fact that he was always hungry; it was to be many years after the war had ended before the constant feeling of hunger finally subsided. Every time Tom informed his mother that he was hungry, she would contradict him and tell him he wasn't. "Go to bed," she would say, "you will feel better in the morning."

He remembered vividly her going berserk one day when he let go of her hand to pick a three-penny piece off the pavement. The fuss she kicked up at the time and the shaking he got ensured he never let go of her again.

Although at the time he did not appreciate the true seriousness of the air raids, Tom knew they were a cause for concern; every time the sirens sounded, to warn of imminent attack, his mother would push him either under the stairs or under the kitchen table. If they were out shopping and an air raid started they would seek refuge in one of the purpose-built shelters or down in one of the underground stations.

Many years later, Tom would reflect on how, as a child, the underground station was always a safe haven – warm and comforting, safe from the bombs and falling buildings – but as he grew into an adult they were to be avoided like the plague to prevent getting blown to bits. The subtle difference between war and terrorism, he supposed.

When he started infant school at the tender age of five, an even more frightening development came into Tom's life, with the arrival of the flying bombs, or doodlebugs, as they became known. These devices came in two forms. With the earlier model you heard the whine of the jet engine as it approached, and everyone dashed for cover. The engine would then suddenly cut out, and after a brief spell of silence, during which everyone prayed like mad, you either heard or felt the explosion.

The later model was more deadly, if slightly less frightening. This time if you heard it coming you were OK, because it travelled faster then sound, it had already exploded by the time the noise reached your ears, a bit like the thunder and lightening effect. The one consolation being that you didn't have to dive under the kitchen table any more in order to minimise the chance of getting to meet your maker.

As the war progressed, everyone became accustomed to the daily interruptions and more or less led a normal life. Underground stations and deep shelters became little communities in their own right, with the more enthusiastic among them providing entertainment for both the children and adults alike, turning the nightly gatherings turning into social events. According to Tom's mother, some of the ladies became too 'sociable' with the few available men around.

It would be five years before the war came to an end in 1945, and life began to get a little easier. Food rationing was to remain for some years to come, however, well into the 1950s in fact, and on a weekly diet of what by modern day standards wouldn't make one decent meal everyone seemed to manage.

For a small boy living in London during the war years, Tom found it, if not exciting, interesting. The various members of the armed forces all looked the same to him, so when he asked British soldiers, "Have you got any gum chum?" – a popular request to men in uniform at that time – he was often quite surprised by their reaction, which was not always pleasant. He soon learnt that it was the Americans who were the bearers of such gifts. They seemed to be able to produce all manner of things that were not available in the shops. These included cigarettes, which were much larger than the British ones, nylon stockings for the ladies, chewing gum, and maybe, if you were lucky, chocolate for the children; sometimes you even managed to wangle a tin of fruit out of them.

Tom quite liked the Americans; they were friendly and generous, especially when his older sisters accompanied him. His father, on the other hand, for some reason seemed to take an immediate dislike to them. The popular slogan at the time being that they were oversexed, overpaid and, worst of all, over here. Apart from that Tom had no problem with them.

Tom did manage to pick up quite a few American expressions that were to stay with him and his generation for life. In those far-off heady days when Britain had its own currency consisting of pounds, shillings and pence – abbreviated to LSD for some strange reason – there were four American dollars to the British pound, and it was not long before five shillings became known as a dollar, and the old half crown – 12½ pence in decimal currency – a half a dollar. Tom also learnt that a broad, or a doll, was slang for a girl and that older ladies were addressed as ma'am, or maaarm as they pronounced it. All expressions that annoyed his father immensely, thereby making them more attractive to an impressionable young Tom, who used them whenever he met any female, be she nine or 90.

Eventually the British soldiers returned home from overseas and the Americans went back to their own country, the women they left behind made their excuses for the unexplained increases in their families and all was forgiven, if not forgotten.

By the time the 1950s had arrived, Tom had become a teenager. Vera Lynn and Bing Crosby were superseded by the likes of Frank Sinatra, Frankie Laine, Alma Cogan and Johnnie Ray plus countless others. The era of the big bands came and went, with Ted Heath and his band being among the most popular.

The famous zoot suit, forerunner of the Teddy Boy outfit had arrived. With its extra long jacket it made the shorter person look as though his legs were only 12in long when viewed from behind, or that he was standing in a hole. That, coupled with the obligatory white silk scarf and Arthur English tie – named after a famous comedian of the time – was considered to be the height of fashion.

Cinemas opened on a Sunday afternoon despite opposition from the church, but only after 4 p.m. Young people had money in their pockets to spend, and for the first time you could buy something you really could not afford by paying for it weekly, as hire purchase made its debut. That is if you could raise the required deposit. Yes, Tom's teenage years were trail blazing and exciting.

The 1960s were hailed as the decade of freedom, free love and fashion, but it was the youth of the 50s that paved the way for all these things after the austerity of the war. With their Teddy Boy suits, DA (ducks arse)-shaped haircuts, and rock and roll music.

By the time the mid-60s arrived Tom had met and married Jenny, he had two young children and was embarking on the exciting prospect of starting his own building company. His was destined to be a long and eventful life, unlike the hundreds of thousands, if not millions of men and women who gave their own lives so that we could all live in a free and just world.

Free, as it turned out in Tom's opinion, for others to screw it all up again, by creating a Britain of sleaze, greed and petty restriction. Health and safety became the new god. It was considered unsafe to allow a person to climb a pair of steps unless someone held them steady, children were no longer allowed to play conkers, or play on hard surfaces. But for some strange reason it was quite in order to cram 90 people every day of the week into a London underground carriage built to hold 30.

The general public became frightened to come to the assistance of anybody in trouble in case they ended up being prosecuted, and others used the health and safety guidelines as an excuse to avoid doing their job properly. The older generation became afraid to go out alone at night for fear of being 'mugged', an expression that was unheard of in Tom's youth. Worse still, the elderly were terrified of having to go into hospital because there was more possibility of them dying from something they contracted while under the care of the National Health Service than if they had taken their chances by remaining at home untreated.

Nothing it seemed would provide such a wonderful opportunity to be difficult with the general public as well as not doing what you were paid to do than the dreaded health and safety.

That is, until they introduced the Data Protection Act, which was to prove even more disastrous.

Tom never dreamt that in his lifetime the well-run and organised public services of his youth would disappear, to be replaced by incompetence, or that free people would be restricted in voicing their views for fear of prosecution. That cameras would watch every aspect of peoples lives, to a far greater extent than any fictional George Orwell prophesies, and he wondered if the sacrifices of so many had been in vain.

3

Billy

Sarah was tingling with excitement; she had managed to position herself in a direct line to the finishing post just as the horses were coming into view. From her vantage point high up in the temporary stand she could just make out the familiar figure of Billy astride the big grey that belonged to her uncle; he was just behind the two leading mares. If Billy could win this last race of the afternoon he would be champion rider for the third time in a row. All he had to do was to keep his cool. Billy was prone to go like a bat out of hell from start to finish, but the big grey needed coaxing, otherwise it would dig its heels in and gallop at its own pace. Sarah had drummed this fact into Billy so many times that at last she felt confident he would obey her orders.

"Go Billy go." The tension was almost too much to bear as the riders thundered towards the finish. Billy was still lying third. What was the matter with him? Unable to control herself any longer, Sarah screamed her instructions. "NOW BILLY, NOW." The big grey lengthened its stride as if sensing the importance of Sarah's command. With nostrils flaring it forced a way past the two leading horses to edge its nose to the front. With the cheers of the gymkhana crowd ringing in his ears Billy raised his arm in a victory salute.

Bantry Bay, in the 20th century, was one of Ireland's most beautiful and picturesque coastal villages. It had not yet developed into the thriving market town it was later to become, and so for 12-year-old Billy O'Connor, or William, as his father insisted he was called, it was boring. Beauty and picturesque, along with peacefulness, were not yet part of his vocabulary, and if they had been, would have featured way down on his list of priorities. Billy much preferred the hustle and bustle of nearby Cork town; where he would often accompany his father when he went there on business.

Not that it was all bad. Bantry had its good points. There was the gymkhana, held each month on the seashore. The church of course played a huge part in the community, as did the village pub, although it would be a few years yet before the pub featured in Billy's itinerary.

Billy's father, Patrick O'Connor, was a devout Catholic, hence the fact that Billy attended church regularly. This was made more attractive for him, first because his friend Sarah was also a member of the faith, like 95% of all Irish families, and secondly, for a small Parish it boasted an active young people's section, which met twice during the week and at weekends in the well equipped parish hall built alongside the presbytery. Far enough away so as not to disturb the priest, but close enough for him to keep an eye on what was going on.

Sarah and Billy were inseparable. Despite being two years older than him, Sarah much preferred his company to any of the girls that lived in the village. Smaller in stature than Billy, despite their age difference, she was considered by most to be quite plain. With short blonde hair that barely covered her ears, a face covered in freckles and a pair of glasses that made her look like something out of a comic book, she could have easily been mistaken for a boy.

Billy on the other hand was well built for his age, 5ft 6 in height. With broad shoulders and an unruly mop of ginger hair he was already attracting the attention of the other local girls. For Sarah Sheridan, however, the most appealing things about Billy were his beautiful clear blue eyes and his beguiling smile.

For Billy the most attractive thing about Sarah was that she wasn't like a girl at all, in fact she was better at climbing trees or playing football than any boy he knew. As for horse riding, well, she was even better than him. It was her love of horses that had brought them together as friends in the first place.

Sarah's uncle Sean was the proprietor of the local riding stables. When Billy had arrived there one Saturday morning to enquire if he could help out with the grooming of the animals in return for some free riding lessons, it had been Sarah who had persuaded her uncle to give Billy a trial run.

Weeks turned into months and the Saturday morning trips round the bay exercising the horses together not only improved their riding skills (Billy was hoping to win his third gymkhana in a row this month), but they had struck up a close friendship. Sarah's father, on the other hand, would have preferred his daughter to be less of a tomboy and spend more time on feminine activities with other girls.

During the summer months when not working with the horses, Billy and Sarah would spend the rest of their time scrambling among the rocks in the bay looking for various life forms or climbing the trees in the churchyard. It was here that they had made a pact to remain best friends forever. Sarah Sheridan, however, did not realise that her parents had other ideas; they had already decided that England offered more opportunities, especially for a teenage girl, and within two months of Sarah pledging her undying friendship to Billy, she had been carted off to London where her father hoped to make his fortune and turn his daughter into a lady.

It would be six years before they met up again and Billy's recollection of Sarah was all but a distant memory. He had reconciled himself to the fact that his future would lie within the church. For as long as he could remember Billy's father had told everybody that his dearest wish was that 'William' would one day become a priest, and as 'William' loved his father, he saw no reason to rock the boat.

Patrick O'Connor spent all his spare time working for the church, and was well respected within the Diocese; indeed it was well known that he was on first-name terms with the bishop. Patrick also kept a tight reign on Billy's social activities, ensuring that although female company was not altogether banned, it was certainly not encouraged, and whenever present, well supervised. For his part Billy could honestly say that despite all the attention he received from them, girls were not his main interest in life. Encouraged by his father, he had studded the teachings of his faith and developed other pastimes. His love of horses had been replaced by a keen interest in sport and a liking for all types of music. Music was the main reason he found himself attending the village dance in the church hall. A new Irish band was making a name for itself and had come to Bantry as part of an Irish tour, before trying their luck in England.

As he stood there in front of the stage listening to the band's latest rendition he heard somebody calling out his name. "Billy, Billy O'Connor, it is you isn't it?" Billy turned round to see who had been calling him.

Standing there, not 6ft away from him was the most beautiful girl Billy had ever seen. About 5ft 6 in height with long blonde hair, she looked like an angel from heaven. Even in the subdued lights of the parish hall, her beauty shone through like a beacon from the crowded dance floor. With trim hips, leading to a slender waist, Billy found himself unable to stop his gaze from travelling up to the open-necked blouse that showed off her body to perfection. And what a body it was! Billy felt his mouth drop open like some village idiot; surely this was not the skinny kid he had known from when he was a boy.

"Stop gawping and come and give me a hug." Billy tore his gaze away from where he sensed he should not be looking to see this vision of loveliness laughing at him, her eyes sparkling with mischief. "Sarah Sheridan, I don't believe it, it is you isn't it, I'm not dreaming."

"You're not dreaming Billy, now come over here and give me that hug."

Billy dashed over and grabbed Sarah round the waist. As he lifted her off her feet and whirled her around, her breasts pushed into his face. "What are you doing here, where have you been these past few years?" he gasped.

"I'm back here for an aunt's funeral, and I've been in England, now stop asking questions and dance with me."

Billy and Sarah danced for most of the night; neither of them, it seemed, realised that the situation had changed from being 'just friends' to something quite different. Things inside were happening to Billy that never happened when they were together as children. He tried to hide his embarrassment from Sarah by dancing with her at arm's length, but each time he moved away, she would grab him and press her perspiring body so close that Billy thought he would die of shame; he was sure everyone in the hall could see his condition. And all the time Sarah was laughing, teasing him in his humiliation.

Immediately the music ended, a much-relieved Billy grabbed Sarah by the hand, desperate to return to his seat. He was anxious to cool off and try to regain his self-control; never before had he experienced such feelings. Seeing Sarah again after all these years had opened up a whole new side to his nature, a side that he was none too sure of controlling.

"Let's go outside, I'm hot in here," pleaded Sarah. Despite his misgivings, Billy allowed himself to be led out into the churchyard where they had played as children. Hand-in-hand together, walking among the gravestones, they chatted about old times; it was as if they had never been apart.

Suddenly Sarah turned and kissed Billy on the mouth long and hard. Feeling him respond, she slid her hand slowly up his inner thigh until she found what she was searching for; its hugeness caught her by surprise and she let out a gasp of excitement. "So you are pleased to see me, Billy Boy?" she laughed.

Before he could answer Sarah dropped to her knees, and in one swift movement unzipped him to reveal the object of her desire. Removing it from its place of safety she grasped him with both hands and began to slowly engulf him.

Something inside Billy was telling him she must stop. He had got to end this madness now, but he was powerless; any second now he knew he would be lost. As he looked down at her he knew instantly that from that moment on, nothing in his life would ever mean as much to him as this moment. Sarah paused; removing herself from him, she gently pulled him down beside her between the gravestones.

"Relax Billy, and think of Ireland." Billy could still feel Sarah gently caressing him as at the same time she removed her pants; in one deft movement she was astride him. Guiding him into her, Sarah began to rock backwards and forwards, gently at first, then more urgently. Billy's mind was in turmoil; nothing like this had ever happened to him before, any second now it would all be over for him, he would be finished before she had started, his embarrassment would be complete. But Sarah's years of horse riding experience were not for nothing; somehow her movements restricted the flow of his juices and he knew he was at her mercy until she was ready.

"Go Billy, go!" Sarah's manner suddenly changed, she almost snapped at him. Together in unison they thrust into each other with a force that almost made them part company, but she held him firmly between her thighs with a grip strengthened by years in the saddle. Sarah was transported back in time, racing round the bay with Billy on a Saturday morning. It was almost unbearable. "Now Billy, now!" she shouted, and with one last crescendo Billy felt his juices surge from him. Sarah cried out as if in pain as the hotness of him burned into her. Suddenly the race was over.

They lay there side-by-side for what seemed an eternity before Sarah released his hand and stood up. Bending over, she kissed him gently on the lips. "Friends forever eh Billy?" she whispered, before quickly disappearing across the churchyard back into the parish hall.

Three months had passed since that night in the graveyard and Billy had received no word from Sarah. He had tried to erase the memory of their night of passion from his mind, but to no avail. Torn between his desire to see her again and his overwhelming guilt, he was at his wits' end as to what to do next. Should he make enquiries to find out if Sarah had returned to England or should he just try and carry on with his life and forget her? Was it his imagination or had his father's attitude to him changed in the last couple of weeks? The doubts within only seemed to confuse him further. In the end Billy would turn to the one thing that was constant in his life – his faith. Not, however, before he had spoken to his father to seek his advice.

Patrick listened in silence as Billy related an extremely censured version of the events that had taken place in the graveyard. He loved him more than anything in this world, ever since Billy's mother had died giving birth to their son. That son was the focal point of Patrick's life, his reason for living. "You must follow your heart," he said, eventually. "I cannot say truthfully that I am not disappointed, but whatever makes you happy in life, will make me happy."

Billy flung his arms around his father and hugged him tightly; at that very moment if he had to choose between his own happiness and that of his father then he would choose the latter. "I think if it is still possible, Dad, I would like to continue my studies and become a priest."

Patrick paused. It was at a time like this that he missed the support and advice of a woman. He was sure in his heart that Billy's brief encounter into carnal knowledge with Sarah Sheridan would be his first and last. "If that's what you truly want, I will have a word with the bishop, but only if you are 100% certain that you can maintain a life of celibacy. Now I think the best thing you can do, William, is go to confession."

4

Lost and Found (out)

'It's Time to Say Goodbye', was the tune that Jenny always said that she wanted played at her funeral to send her on her way. Tom had sat there for nearly an hour, half listening to somebody he had never met, and worse still, someone who had never met Jenny, going on and on about her life. But then he supposed situations like this were commonplace in this day and age; nobody seemed to take the time to get to know anyone properly anymore, least of all the church. The only thing they were interested in these days was how much you put in the offertory box. Tom had only been half listening anyway; he was too preoccupied with his feelings of guilt to pay too much attention to some over-sincere cleric. Jenny's chosen music had jolted him back to reality.

The two boys had been a tower of strength since Jenny died; he could feel their presence either side of him as he sat there, completely lost in his own thoughts. Without them Tom didn't know how he would have coped. As the music came to an end and the cleric furtively pushed the button to activate the mechanism that would take Jenny on her final journey and out of Tom's life forever, it was all Tom could do to stop himself from running after her. It was the sound that halted him in his tracts; for one brief moment it was as if somebody was opening their garage door.

A feeling of immense relief washed over Tom as he entered the house. At last he could see some light at the end of the tunnel. For months now he had been trying to break it to Fiona gently that it was time to put an end to their affair, but each time he tried to raise the subject she would burst into tears and because he was so completely helpless when it came to dealing with her, they would end up in bed together. This time, however, things had been different. Fiona had been in a strange mood from the moment he had arrived, something was obviously troubling her. When Tom asked what the matter was she became very aggressive and demanded to know if he intended to leave Jenny or not. Grasping the opportunity, Tom explained that he would never leave Jenny, despite how close they had become over the months. Jenny was his reason for living; no way was he going to hurt her if he could avoid it, and he certainly wasn't going to leave her.

It had not been pleasant, but he had done it. As Tom closed the front door he could still feel the emotional effects of his and Fiona's last encounter, but this time he had resisted her pleas to make love for "just one more time" and instead had spent the past two hours driving around aimlessly before going home. Was it possible to love two women at the same time? Tom was sure that it was, and if it wasn't he had come pretty close. If he had not ended it there and then that afternoon, deep down Tom knew he would never have ended it. Fiona had a hold on him that when he was in her company all sense of rhyme or reason, or even morality went out of the window, and yet when he was back with Jenny, the feeling of guilt over his unfaithfulness was unbearable. But not unbearable enough to make him end his clandestine relationship. That was until that afternoon.

At last Tom was back home to his beloved Jenny, to make up for all the deceit and lies. They could now continue to live their lives in peace and harmony; Jenny need never know he had been unfaithful. Tom called out as he closed the door behind him. The house was strangely silent as he made his way along the hall into the lounge. Tom called out again. "Are you there, sweetheart?"

Jenny was sitting in the half-light as Tom entered the lounge, her arms wrapped round her legs, which were tucked up under her chin. Tom could see straight away that she had been crying. "What's up, sweetheart, aren't you feeling well?" There was a sinking feeling in the pit of Tom's stomach as he forced himself not to panic.

"FEELING WELL? FEELING WELL?" Jenny's voice was almost screaming. "Oh I'm feeling fucking well alright. I've just spent the last two hours finding out that my husband keeps his brains in his trousers and has been shagging all and sundry for the last six months. Is that all you can say, 'aren't you feeling well?' By the way, in case the penny hasn't dropped yet, I've had a visit this afternoon from your friend Fiona Philips."

The weeks turned into months and still Tom's relationship with Jenny showed no sign of improving. He had been banished to the spare room, and even the kids were ignoring him. The more he tried to explain what for him was impossible to put into words, the more Jenny probed into his reasons for betraying her. But there were no reasons. OK, Jenny had been tired and stressed lately, but that was just an excuse Tom had thought up to relieve him of the guilt. No! Deep down he was the arsehole and he knew it.

Tom decided it would be best if he kept well away from the Philips' residence. In moments of deep depression and self-pity he had been tempted to drive by the house and see if he could snatch a glimpse of Fiona, but even at his lowest ebb Tom knew that if Jenny found out, it would end any hope of his marriage returning to some sort of normality, he would lose her forever. In the end Tom could resist no longer. Something inside him kept nagging away as to the reason Fiona had tried to destroy him by revealing all to Jenny. He knew there would be no peace of mind for him until he had asked her why.

Tom could hardly believe his eyes; the Philips place looked deserted, the windows were bare apart from some grubby net curtains, and there was an estate agents' 'Sold' board nailed to the front gate. Tom parked a discreet distance away from the house and walked back to investigate. There was no sign of life. It was possible that they hadn't moved out yet; he knew if he ran into Peter all hell would be let loose, but he had to find out why Fiona had revealed their affair to Jenny. Throwing all caution to the wind Tom entered the front gate and walked up the side of the house past the garage, a journey he had made on so many occasions while Peter had been playing golf. The 'up and over' garage door was slightly open, Tom, could see at a glance it had been forced; it didn't take long these days for the local villains to suss out when a place was empty. Tom made his way round the back of the house and peered through the window. He remembered the first time he had made that journey. Was that Fiona he could hear hoovering away? No, the house was definitely empty. The kitchen was bare except for the lone table, standing there mocking him as he craned his neck, searching for signs of life.

Tom decided it was time to leave. Maybe the new owners would be arriving soon; if they found him wandering about he would have a lot of explaining to do. As he walked back along the side of the house past the garage, Tom could not resist one last look inside. He managed to force the already-damaged 'up and over' door open just enough to allow himself to squeeze inside. His emotions were all over the place, a chapter of his life had come to an end and somehow he was finding it hard to accept.

It's funny how even a garage can look eerie and deserted when the occupants move out of a house. The old single wardrobe that Peter once used to keep his garden tools and golf equipment in had been vandalised; one door had been completely broken off its hinges and tossed aside, the contents that used to be so neatly arranged on the shelves were strewn all over the floor and someone had opened a tin of paint and daubed it all over the walls. Tom sighed as he surveyed the wanton damage. The garage had been Peter's pride and joy, the place where he spent time cleaning his clubs and shoes, and planned his next round of golf. It was also the place where Tom had once made love to Fiona one wet afternoon while Peter was inside watching sport on television. Tom's mind was working overtime. How could he have let his feelings for Fiona completely take over his life? Determined to block all further thoughts of the Philips' household from his mind, he turned to leave. It was then that Tom saw the message written on the back of the garage door. The writing had almost disappeared except for his name, which seemed to jump out at him as he craned his neck to read the barely visible words.

'Tom please forgive me, I am so sorry. I will love you forever, be happy.'

Out in the fresh air Tom struggled to control his emotions. So Fiona had acted on a whim. In the end she had regretted revealing all to Jenny. If only he could turn the clock back to the time he had told Fiona he had no intention of leaving Jenny, he felt sure he could have handled it differently. But then diplomacy had never been his strong point. Why on earth had he given Fiona the impression that she was of no great importance in his life when in fact quite the opposite was the case? Well it was too late now; he had gambled and lost. The only thing to do was to try and make it up to Jenny.

*

"Are you all right, Dad? It's time to go home."

Tom could feel the boys helping him up from his seat as he returned from his brief journey into the past. Tradition dictated that the immediate family were the first to leave the tiny chapel and shake hands with the presiding minister as they left; Tom would have preferred to have remained behind and spent a few minutes alone with his beloved Jenny, trying to expunge his guilt.

If Tom thought Jenny's funeral service was never going to end, it was nothing to the wake. Where did all these people come from? Tom barely recognised any of them, even though apparently most of them were his own grandchildren. Kids today seemed to grow up faster than ever, one minute they were running about in nappies, the next they reappeared 6ft tall and had acquired deep voices. Not only that, they were wandering all over the house poking their noses into things that were none of their business. And the questions! "Are you going to be all right Granddad?" "Are you going to carry living in the house Granddad?" "Did Grandma leave a will, Granddad."

In the end Tom could stand it no longer. "Yes I am, I don't know, and no she didn't, so will you all piss off home and leave me in peace."

Gradually, one by one, either through boredom or a feeling that they had done their duty, everyone began to drift off home, to carry on with their own lives, leaving Tom to his memories. The house seemed strangely empty without Jenny; somehow it had lost its warmth. And now that the funeral was over it suddenly dawned on Tom that for the first time in over 60 years he was completely alone.

5

The Home

Arriving at the home for the first time as a resident, Tom surveyed his surroundings. So this was where he would live out the rest of his days. Although he had visited Sea View many times before, the final decision as to whether or not he wanted to take up permanent residence had still been a traumatic experience. This would be the last move he ever made, the place which in effect he had chosen to die. He had hoped that when the time came for him to shuffle off this mortal coil, he would be among family and friends. Well, Tom had outlived all his friends, and without Jenny the family had suddenly lost its importance to him. There was a strange air of finality about the whole affair.

Jenny's death had hit Tom harder than he was prepared to admit. He could not imagine life without her; the last few months had brought home to him just how much he had relied on her. Well with a bit of luck he would soon be joining her, and then it wouldn't matter if he had made the right decision or not.

At least the place was clean, and everyone since his arrival so far had been pleasant to him. Tom thought that that in itself indicated the home was being managed properly.

The Afro Caribbean girl who had introduced herself as Pearl seemed kind enough, her smile was warm and friendly and she had the knack of putting people at their ease. In some strange way she reminded Tom of Jenny; she certainly was beautiful. Tom's thoughts once again reverted to Jenny. It was all he could do to stop himself from bursting into tears. He must make an effort to stop dwelling on the past; what would this young girl think if every time she spoke to him he ended up crying his eyes out?

A large double-fronted Victorian house set in what by today's standards would be called spacious grounds, Sea View gave one the feeling that it belonged in a more gracious and bygone age. The steeply pitched grey-slated roof with its twin gables somehow seemed to give the impression that the building was somewhat larger than it actually was. The dull red brickwork, prominent in so many South of England coastal towns, were covered in the ever-searching tentacles of a giant wisteria, that in the summer transformed the building from its rather austere winter appearance into a magical castle in the sky, floating in a sea of blue. The two square shaped bays on the ground floor, devoid of curtains, allowed passers-by to peer in at the occupants as they partook of their daily sustenance in the dining room, or wave to the pale faces peering out from the adjacent lounge. The upper bay windows by contrast were adorned with brightly coloured blinds to give the occupants a feeling of being part of the outside world, but at the same time ensuring their privacy. The only concession to the modern world was the removal of part of the front boundary wall and the construction of a driveway to allow local tradesmen access to the rear of the premises and to accommodate the private ambulance discreetly parked round the back of the building.

The room Tom had chosen was large; he had made sure of that before making his decision to move in. No way was he going to be locked up in a box for the rest of his life, even if it was only for a short while.

Tom's family, such as it was these days with most of them living abroad, had been quite helpful in that respect. They had insisted it was written into his contract with the home that he occupied the same room for the rest of his days unless he decided to move out. But at the age of 80 that was highly unlikely. The premium paid for this arrangement had been quite high, but well worth it. As his son had said at the time, you can't take it with you, Dad, so enjoy it while you can.

As one of the few units on the ground floor, Tom's room was the only one to have an en-suite containing a shower and toilet, which led him to believe that in all probability it was originally built to house a member of the staff. If there was one thing that Tom dreaded more than anything else, when making up his mind whether or not to move into Sea View, it was that he would have to share the basic facilities with a load of other old people. Throughout his whole life Tom had been a very private person when it came to such matters. The room also boasted a pair of casement doors, which led out into spacious grounds dotted here and there with sets of garden furniture. As he stepped through them he could smell the sea air and hear the faint sound of the waves pounding the shore. This will do for me, he thought to himself, before moving back inside to search out the communal lounge.

The name 'Sea View Care and Rest Home', if you wanted to be pedantic, was an offence against the Trade Description Act, because it was a good five minutes' walk to the sea. However, when the name was originally chosen, probably towards the end of the 20th century when the building was converted into a retirement home, it could well have been a true statement. But nowadays, what with all the new premises built up around it, that was no longer the case.

Sea View had space for 20 to 25 residents, depending how many were prepared to share a room. The Local Authority-sponsored residents were never a problem; they were grateful for a bed in what was predominately a private home. The private fee payers, however, were a little fussier, unless they felt lonely, then they were quite happy to share. With a large lounge, a well-designed dining room leading to a surprisingly well-equipped kitchen, it was all that the retired gentry required. There was also an annexe built in the grounds of the home containing two separate medical wards, in the event of anybody needing special attention, together with staff accommodation in the form of two bedsits, one of which was occupied by Pearl, the other by one of the other nurses. All in all it was a well-run self-sufficient home and Tom thought he would be quite content once he had settled in.

Entering the lounge, Tom stood momentarily in the doorway and looked around the room. It was occupied by several small groups of people either playing cards or chatting among themselves, with the exception of one chap who was sitting alone, staring out of the window.

As he ventured further into the room, Tom noticed a man on the far side of the room holding court with a group of women who seemed to be hanging on to his every word. He glanced up as Tom drew level, and their eyes met. Tom smiled and nodded. To his irritation the man completely ignored him. Raising his voice he carried on with his conversation. Well, fuck you too, Tom said to himself and walked on.

A quartet of ladies looked up from their card came and smiled briefly as he passed. By the time he had reached the other side of the room the solitary man, sensing Tom approaching, tore his gaze away from the window and stood up and offered his hand in greeting.. "Good morning I'm Robert Downing, fellow resident. Welcome aboard."

Tom grasped the outstretched hand. The grip was warm and firm for a man of his years. "Tom Hall; just arrived, nice to meet you." And so started a friendship that was to last for nearly 15 years.

Toms first evening alone in his room seemed endless; it was far worse than anything he had experienced since sleeping on his own for the first time after losing Jenny. He had barely had more than a couple of hours of uninterrupted sleep throughout the whole night. If it wasn't somebody moving about in the corridor outside, it was the sound of the sea pounding against the breakwaters. Funny how the faint sound of the waves from earlier in the day, which he found so pleasant, were magnified out of all proportion at night, so that they appeared to be beating against his very door. Then when he did drop off for a moment there were the dreams. Faces from the past. Charlie pointing an accusing finger, Peter Philips with tears streaming down his face asking him why. But above all there was Jenny with that hurt look in her eyes, the look that tore his heart to pieces and filled him with guilt.

Tom cried out to her for forgiveness, and the sound of his own voice jolted him into wakefulness, but there was nobody there. He buried his head deep into his pillow as he tried to obliterate the images from his mind; it was soaking wet with the perspiration brought about by his torment. Was this going to be how he was destined to live out the rest of his days; in a never-ending nightmare?

At last the dawn broke. Tom had spent the past two hours pacing up and down trying to avoid sleep at any cost. Soon it would be time to join the other residents for breakfast; he couldn't wait.

Entering the dining room that morning, Tom could not help noticing that the make-up of the little groups of people he had seen the day before were still as he had first seen them. The man who had ignored him was still holding court, only this time he was waving his cereal spoon around as if conducting his own orchestra, and the ladies' card school, instead of dealing cards, were handing out slices of toast to each other.

Robert was sitting alone in the corner as Tom walked over and enquired if he could join him. "Feel free, I'll be glad of the company." They breakfasted together and Tom began to realise that Robert was really a very private person. While he was quite happy for Tom to tell him about his own life, he gave very little away about himself. He had been in the home for around 18 months, and at some time in his life Tom got the impression that he had been in show business. But every time Tom probed a little deeper, Robert steered the conversation in a different direction. He was, however, pleased to learn that Tom liked to walk as often as he could. "Maybe we can walk to the front together and sit and watch the world go by?"

When it came to the other residents, Robert was a little more informative. Apparently most of them were women, their main interests, apart from gossiping it seemed, were playing cards or knitting. "I'm not sure how old they think they are," he laughed, but the majority of them knit baby clothes.

"How about 'God's gift to women' over there?" asked Tom, nodding in the direction of the guy that had snubbed him the night before.

"Oh, that's Brigadier Jack Holland; he won the Falklands war single-handed, or so he tells his entourage. Nasty piece of work if you ask me. There's something about him that doesn't quite add up, something that I can't put my finger on. Have you tried speaking to him yet? If you do he will probably ignore you."

"Then I won't give him the chance," replied Tom.

They finished their breakfast, chatting idly about all and sundry when Robert got up to leave. "I hope we can be friends, Tom, it gets bloody lonely in here sometimes."

"I'd like that. See you lunchtime maybe?"

"It's a date. By the way, I suppose it's too much to ask if you play chess?"

"I do actually," replied Tom.

"We must get together for a game some time, maybe after lunch perhaps?"

And so Tom settled in and for the next few years he and Robert developed a routine of walks along the seafront, the odd game of chess, and endless conversations about what was wrong with the world, but above all forged a deep and lasting friendship.

Pearl entered the dining room just as Tom and Robert were leaving. It was nice to see that Robert had found a friend at last, instead of sitting there gazing out of the window all day long. Perhaps now he would open up a little bit and join in with the others.

Male residents were few and far between these days, apart from Brigadier Jack Holland, Robert, and now Tom; that was the extent of their presence at Sea View. Unfortunately in Pearl's opinion Jack Holland was an unpleasant type of man. The way he looked at her at certain times made her feel uncomfortable. He was forever boasting of his wartime experiences and of his success with the opposite sex. Robert on the other hand had always been the perfect gentleman in all his dealings with her.

Tom Hall, the new chap, seemed nice enough, although Pearl suspected that deep down he was a troubled soul. When making her rounds during the night she was sure that she had heard the sound of someone sobbing coming from the vicinity of his room.

Pearl decided to keep an eye on Tom Hall; she knew that he had only recently lost his wife and was therefore probably feeling very vulnerable.

He also reminded her of her own grandfather, with that mischievous twinkle in his eye. Although she had only known Tom for a very short while, unlike when she was dealing with Brigadier Jack Holland, Pearl felt comfortable in his company.

"What made you decide to take up residence at Sea View, Tom?"

Tom glanced up from the chessboard; Robert was looking at him intently waiting for an answer to his question. Tom thought for a while before answering. "Well, I suppose in the end it was the washing machine." Seeing Robert's puzzled expression, Tom laughed. It was funny now but it wasn't at the time. "For the first few weeks, although I missed Jenny like mad, I was managing. The boys would pop in to check up on me and see that everything was OK, and Margaret our neighbour was very good. We had all more or less grown up together over the years so we were used to helping one another out in times of strife. But when Margaret suddenly decided she couldn't cope on her own any longer and was going to move in with her daughter, that's when I decided I had to make friends with the washing machine." Robert was looking even more confused as Tom continued. "Well, it had been one of those weeks really. I had got myself into a bit of a state right from the moment I opened my eyes that morning. Lying there in the early hours I was gasping for a cup of tea, I thought, Jenny will get up in a minute and make one, but there was no sign of movement so I stretched out my leg to make contact, like I have done ever since the day we got married. There was no one there, of course, only a cold empty space. I think that was one of the hardest things I have had to accept since Jenny died. That and our little chat each morning as we planned our day. Then the magic box stopped working."

Robert couldn't resist. "The magic box?"

"Yes, for as long as I can remember I have put all my dirty shirts, socks, underpants and anything else that needed washing into the linen box under the bay window, and low and behold, as if by magic, the following day they would reappear – washed, ironed and put away in their rightful places. It was a private joke that Jenny and I shared. Now all that had come to an end; the box was overflowing with dirty washing and I hadn't got a clue what to do about it, but I knew I had to do something. Apart from the problem of the magic box, there was also the question of stocking up with food. I had been managing on what was in the house, but now things were beginning to run out. Jenny had always dealt with that sort of thing. I had no idea whether we had salted or unsalted butter, smoked or unsmoked bacon, the list was endless. Anyway, as I said, I decided to stock up with the necessities and sort out the washing.

Even then nothing seemed to go right. When I returned from my trip to the shops I found I had locked myself out. I have always been careless with keys. As I peered through the letterbox, calling out for Jenny to open the door, I could see them sitting there on the hall table. It was only because Margaret came out to see what all the fuss was about that I was able to get back indoors. Jenny had given her a spare key in case of such an emergency. Back inside the house, I gathered up all the dirty washing ready to make a start, but I couldn't open the machine door. Ten minutes later, more by luck than judgement, I pushed a little half-concealed lever and it sprung open. My first attempt at using the machine didn't turn out too bad really, if you discount all the foam over the kitchen floor, and I was sure that none of my shirts were pink. The second load was the one that made me realise that I was fighting a losing battle when it came to looking after myself, as well as keep the house running smoothly, like it always did when Jenny was around.

I started off well enough; after filling the machine up with all my dirty jumpers and anything else I could find, like I had seen Jenny do, I bunged in the washing powder and softener, switched the machine on and sat back and waited. Everything appeared to be going along fine until after about an hour, when suddenly the machine stopped. I must have spent nearly all morning trying to find out what was wrong and to get my washing out of the machine. Eventually I managed to force open the door of the blasted contraption, only to discover that that was the last thing I should have done. Hot water spilled all over the kitchen floor, followed by the half-completed wash. I slipped on the wet tiles, banged my head on the kitchen table nearly knocking my brains out, and to cap it all, when I did gather my senses and start to clean up the mess, I found all my jumpers had shrunk so much that they wouldn't fit a five-year-old.

It was at that moment I decided that I needed looking after properly. So with the help of my two boys I made the necessary arrangements and moved into here."

Robert laughed. "Well, I did ask. A simple 'I was fed up with being on my own' would have sufficed. But it's an ill wind. At least I've gained a friend, and I get a game of chess thrown in as a bonus."

6

The Branigans

Joseph and Colleen Branigan had been married now for ten years or more, during which time they had been extremely happy with rarely a crossed word between them. Colleen was a primary school teacher, specialising in children with learning difficulties and Joseph a qualified engineer in the construction industry. Between them they were able to enjoy a comfortable lifestyle, free from the financial worries that beset most couples.

Despite their financial success, however, they were not completely content. Their life lacked the one thing they craved for most of all – a child. Despite all their efforts to produce an offspring of their own they had been unsuccessful and were beginning to come to terms with the fact that they would remain childless. Deep down, Joseph was convinced that he was the main cause of their problem. As a teenager he had contracted mumps and suspected that he might be sterile, or as his colleagues at work teased, firing blanks. He had, unlike his beautiful wife, never been terribly interested in the physical side of their marriage, preferring to concentrate more on the financial aspect of it.

Colleen, on the other hand, had no hang-ups as regards to sex. For her it was a very important part of her marriage. If she could be granted one wish in life, apart from being able to produce a child of her own, it would be that Joseph was more active in the bedroom. She had tried her best to encourage him, but her efforts only seemed to make matters worse. Colleen wondered if this might be part of their problem – was she too intimidating for Joseph? He could rarely last the course these days when they made love, and more often than not lately he couldn't even get started. She had decided recently to adopt a more placid approach to their lovemaking and try to be less demanding; however, so far she was not having much success.

It was Joseph who began the process that changed their lives. As they were both staunch Catholics he suggested they seek advice from the church. He was quite prepared to consider adoption, even though he knew Colleen wasn't too keen. At least the church would ensure that any adoptive child came from a good Catholic background, and who knows, in time, when the pressure was off, they might find they were able to produce an offspring of their own. The other option of course was to seek medical advice. But being aware of the church's views regarding the use of so-called artificial methods in these matters, Colleen was less enthusiastic. So it was with mixed feelings that she agreed to Joseph's suggestion.

Father William O'Connor listened quietly to the problems of the couple in front of him. He had only arrived at their church a week ago, straight from the seminary, and felt he lacked the experience to judge such matters. His recent ordination had proved to be a very emotional affair attended by his ailing father, and he had not yet got used to the idea of being a fully-fledged priest. It was not even his parish. The incumbent priest, Father Stephen Finn, was away on ecclesiastical business and William was only there as a temporary measure. They seemed a God-fearing couple, however, and he was determined to do his best to help them with their problem. Although William wasn't too keen on the idea of investigating the possibility of artificial means to help Colleen conceive, the last thing he wanted when Father Finn returned was to find out he had encouraged this couple down a path that offended the incumbent priest.

After explaining to them as best as he could that it would be prudent for the time being if they learnt to relax and put their trust in God, Father William turned his attention to Joseph; he was obviously a hard working individual if somewhat on the shy side. William could see how being married to a vivacious woman like Colleen would at times eat away at a man's confidence when it came to matters of the flesh. Maybe it might help if Joseph eased up on the work and found himself a hobby. The occasional fishing weekend, perhaps. He reminded him that it wasn't a sin to have the occasional drink in the local pub once or twice a week. That in itself should boost Joseph's confidence.

Turning to Colleen, Father William realised just how inexperienced he was. The vows he had recently undertaken included giving up the sins of the flesh and it disturbed him slightly that he found her so bubbly and attractive. She rekindled memories of his past, of someone he thought had been erased from his mind forever. He was finding it difficult to concentrate and the more he tried to block out these memories, the more they returned to haunt him. William suspected in his heart that he was fighting a losing battle.

Colleen for her part was totally relaxed with the situation as she related the intimate details of their marriage to her priest; for her it was no different than going to confession. She did notice that this young priest seemed tense; surely he was not embarrassed by her disclosures. Maybe it was because he lacked the experience of Father Finn. Come to think of it, Father William was quite handsome. Colleen thought he was probably in his mid 20s, with lovely clear blue eyes and the most engaging of smiles. Underneath that rather drab cassock she sensed dwelt a healthy virile body. What a waste. Yes, Father William was quite a dish, unlike her usual priest.

It was obvious to Father William that Colleen was the more dominant half of the partnership and he decided she needed guidance of a different nature than he had given to Joseph. Obviously a woman of strong character and boundless energy, she would have to learn to play a less active roll in her marriage. He felt Colleen, like Joseph, needed something to take her mind off of their problems.

On their journey home Joseph and Colleen discussed the meeting with Father William and agreed that the advice that they had been given was sound and that they should act upon it. It was decided Joseph would take up fishing and spend at least one evening a week down at the local pub in the company of his male friends.

Colleen, as suggested, would help Father William within the church in her spare time, either arranging the flowers or helping him with his office work until he settled in or Father Stephen returned.

Since starting her church duties, Colleen had changed dramatically; not only had she become more passive in their relationship, but there was an air of contentment about her that Joseph was sure had only developed since she began working with Father William.

For his part Joseph was certainly more relaxed these days. Colleen had stopped harassing him in the bedroom department, which in turn had given him an added interest in her; in fact, their last attempt at lovemaking had been the most successful for months. This, coupled with his recent leisure activities, had boosted his ego enormously.

Colleen enjoyed her spare time working for the church, what with Joseph either spending the weekend fishing, or down at the local pub, life would have been dull and lonely without something to occupy her mind. She also enjoyed the company of Father William; when he switched off from being a priest he could be quite fun. Colleen was genuinely surprised by his knowledge of popular music and current trends among the young. So unlike the recently returned Father Stephen Finn, who being a member of the old school, had no interest in such matters, and had no hesitation in voicing his disapproval at the closeness that had developed between her and Father William.

It was this disapproval that Colleen felt sure was the reason why William had been trying to avoid her lately. Each time she tried to engage him in conversation in anything other than church matters he mumbled his excuses and left the room.

Father Stephen Finn was visiting an old school friend in Dublin. He would be away from his parish for a couple of days and had left Father William in charge during his absence, with strict instructions to keep all contact with Colleen Branigan to a minimum. Their apparent closeness disturbed him. Despite William's assurance that nothing untoward had happened or was ever likely to happen between them he was still nervous. He decided that as soon as he returned he would persuade Colleen to give up her voluntary duties within the parish and return to a life of looking after her husband.

William finished counting the weekend offering before deciding to take a shower. He was alone in the presbytery for the first time in weeks. Father Stephen had buggered off to see his old school friend and left him in sole charge, albeit with precise conditions.

What a relief it was standing there with the hot water cascading over his body. William could feel himself responding to the heat as his mind drifted back in time, and he closed his eyes and thought of Sarah. The vows William had so recently undertaken were of paramount importance to him; without them his life would have no purpose, but they were so difficult to adhere to, the hardest of all the vow of celibacy.

William gained enormous comfort from the knowledge that he had fulfilled his father's dearest wish and had become a priest. Only at this very moment did the extent of his sacrifice to God seem unbearable.

Even with the hot water beating against his face when he lifted his head, William could taste the salt from the tears streaming from him as he indulged in self-gratification.

Colleen appeared deep in thought as she prepared the flowers for the weekend church services. It was no longer the pleasure that it used to be before Father Stephen came back from his seminar, in fact she felt quite miserable. Father William seemed so distant these past few days, as if other things preoccupied his mind. By rights Colleen shouldn't be in the church today; Joseph had entered a fishing competition for the day and she didn't want to be at home on her own.

The sound of someone descending the stairs that led from the presbytery to the church made Colleen look up from her task. As the door to the vestry opened, the figure of a man holding a large bag of money in each hand stood framed in the doorway. His sudden appearance startled Colleen and she was about to cry out for assistance when she realised that the intruder was Father William. Instinctively she stepped back into the shadows.

Unaware that he was not alone, William entered the vestry with his bathrobe agape, displaying his naked body for the entire world to see. He was in a much better frame of mind now that he was refreshed; the shower had fulfilled its purpose and he felt like a new man. Even as the warm air from the church displaced his open robe he could feel his firmness returning. William was unconcerned; there was nobody around to disturb him. For a few moments longer he could be Billy again.

It was difficult to know who was the most surprised as their eyes met. William dropped the offertory bags and held up his hands in horror, in sudden realisation that he was displaying

45

his nakedness to a female member of the parish, but oblivious to the fact that his reaction had made matters worse.

Colleen momentarily recoiled in panic before quickly gathering her senses; she might never have this opportunity again. Stepping forward she skilfully pulled William's robe together in a half-hearted attempt to conceal his embarrassment. Placing her hand inside the still slightly opened robe Colleen searched for him while kissing him gently on the lips.

The weeks had flown by and turned into months since Joseph and Colleen had first sought advice from their priest. Things could not have worked out better for them. Not only had the physical side of their marriage improved beyond all expectations, but also Colleen's personality had changed dramatically. She had at last calmed down and become the more passive half of the partnership. There was an air of contentment about her that Joseph put down to the influence of Father William.

The news Joseph received that morning completed his happiness. Colleen had phoned him from their doctor's surgery in a state of high excitement to inform him that she was pregnant. Joseph immediately pleaded with her to give up all her work, including her church duties, in order to avoid a miscarriage. He was somewhat surprised how easily she gave in to his demands; perhaps the prospect of motherhood had calmed her down.

Within the year their happiness was complete. Colleen Branigan gave birth to a beautiful 8 lb baby girl with gingery hair and the most beautiful clear blue eyes. Their trust in God had been rewarded. The Lord had provided. Martha May Branigan was baptised in the local parish church on August 18th 1991 by Father William O'Connor, his final act before being moved to a new parish, as strongly recommended to the church hierarchy by Father Stephen Finn.

7

Pearl

Looking at her as she walked along the seafront, by any standards Pearl Bakewell was, to say the least, a beautiful woman. Thirty-two years of age, she had not yet found a man that lived up to her expectations, so had remained single, much to the consternation of her mother, Joyce Bakewell.

Joyce was forever trying to marry Pearl off to every eligible man that her daughter ever brought home. "When are you going to make me a grandmother?" Joyce would ask in that fake Jamaican accent she put on when things weren't to her liking. She would go on and on. "And me a midwife, what would Nanny and Granddad have thought? Let alone Great Grandpa and Myrtle?"

The constant barrage was endless. I wish my mother would make up her mind, Pearl fumed in her more depressed moments. One minute she's ranting on about becoming a grandmother, the next, when she knows I am meeting a new young man, she tells me to make sure I keep my knees together. Well, she had kept her knees together for 32 years, and if the truth was known, her past experiences with men had been very unpleasant and now she was finding it difficult to form any kind of relationship with them.

Pearl often thought that if she got herself pregnant by the next man that came along it would serve her mother right, then

47

she really would have cause to revert to her phoney Caribbean accent. Pearl knew she never would, of course; that was part of her problem. Anyhow, she had more respect for herself. Besides, the nursing home took up most of her time and since joining the local church choir there was hardly any time for anything else.

She had high hopes of the choir, but she wasn't going to mention anything to her mother. Not yet anyway. No point in setting her off again until it was absolutely necessary.

The young man in question had joined the choir at the same time as Pearl and they'd hit if off straight away. Although he was not what Pearl would call handsome, he was by no means ugly. Tall by her standard, some 5 ft 10 or 11, well built and with the most beautiful baritone voice she had heard for a long time.

The weather on that first day at the end of choir practice had been awful; it hadn't stopped raining all evening and Malcolm had offered her a lift. As he dropped her off at the retirement home he had leaned across and kissed her on the cheek. Sensing her stiffen at physical contact he had backed off and wished her goodnight. That was a month ago now and things were progressing nicely; they had been out to dinner a couple of times and Malcolm had invited her to eat at his place, hoping it would develop into more than just a meal, but he was determined not to rush things.

Pearl was fourth generation descendant from Jamaican immigrants, her great grandparents having arrived in Tilbury, England, in 1948 aboard the now famous HMS Empire Windrush, and it was a source of great pride that she could boast to all her friends of her family's connection with such an historical event.

Apart from the odd holiday to see her grandparents, she had rarely visited Jamaica, considering herself to be English through and through. This, however, did not stop her from being immensely proud of her ancestry.

As a small girl she remembered sitting on her great grandfather's knee as he related for the umpteenth time how he and his wife Myrtle (Pearl's great grandmother) had made the momentous and painful decision to leave their beloved Jamaica.

With high unemployment and near starvation at home, and a young 14-year-old daughter (Pearl's grandmother), they had had little choice. This did not stop them from lying awake night after night agonising over whether or not they were doing the right thing. Carmen, their daughter, had many friends and was about to leave school; in England it was possible she would have to continue her education for a further two years. But above all she did not want to leave Jamaica.

The decision was made, however, and they had all arrived together in England to find the weather and the natives not very welcoming, in spite of being told before they left their own country that the streets of London were paved with gold and that they would be welcomed with open arms.

Great Grandpa had laughed as he recalled how in the beginning he and Myrtle wore thick heavy overcoats and scarves, even on the sunniest of days, while all the white boys walked about in their shirtsleeves. They had soon realised why all the houses had brick chimneystacks with little red pipes on the top of them. It was because it was so bloody cold in England the natives had to set their houses on fire in order to keep warm. But they eventually got used to the weather, and most of the natives began to accept them.

Finding employment, Grandpa working for London Transport as a conductor on the buses and Myrtle as a cleaner in the garage, they soon began to settle in to their adopted country. Grandpa joined the union and soon became one of its officers looking after the welfare of his fellow Jamaican and Caribbean brothers.

Pearl still smiled as she remembered Grandpa telling her how at each union meeting the convenor would stand up and welcome "our coloured brothers" and he in turn would thank him for the welcome but point out that "we are not your coloured brothers; we are neither green, blue nor yellow; we are black; we are your black brothers".

As Pearl approached the pier she noticed Tom sitting on one of the many benches that were spread along the promenade. He was in deep conversation with Robert Downing. Somehow, that made her feel more content. The pair of them had been friends ever since Tom's arrival at the home all those years ago, but in the last couple of days the atmosphere had suddenly changed between them. She guessed it had been a tiff over something minor. It was good to see that they were back together again. For people of their age, especially men, it was difficult to find friends.

It was a good many years now since Grandpa and Myrtle had passed away but the memory of them still gave her a warm glow. She was glad that in the end, the proceeds Grandpa and Myrtle had received from the little house they had sold in Brixton, South London, together with his old age and transport pensions, had been enough to allow them to sell up and return to Jamaica where they lived out the rest of their lives in comfort.

Pearl's great grandparents had worked hard and received many setbacks since they'd come to Britain. Not least when their daughter Carmen managed to get herself pregnant within two years of their arrival. And upon giving birth to Pearl's mother, Joyce, had left them with her baby and returned to Jamaica, the place she still considered was her true home. By the time Carmen eventually settled down and married, Joyce was attending primary school and remained with her grandparents.

Yes, Pearl had come a long way since leaving London and joining the care home staff in Eastbourne. Her natural affinity and understanding of the elderly had stood her in good stead; she was senior nurse, answerable only to Martha Branigan. Indeed, Pearl had been informed that should Martha ever decide to leave her present position, she was the obvious replacement.

Of her father Pearl remembered very little. He had apparently met and married her mother in the year 2000 and very shortly after that she was born. Within a further eight months he had run off with somebody else and her mother rarely spoke about him, and when she did, it was only in a derogatory way. She did, however, retain his surname so Pearl thought there must still be some feeling there.

8

Death

It was not often Tom had a meal in his room. Under normal circumstances he would join the others in the communal dining area. Apart from the company, you could always glean little bits of information about one of the members of staff. But it wasn't the same without Robert, and today was one of those days when he preferred to be on his own.

It had only been a few weeks since Pauline, one of the old ladies, had been looking out of her window in the early hours of the morning when she had seen a man leaving from either Mary or Pearl's accommodation in the annexe. Tom hadn't been able to discover whether one of them had been entertaining a male guest overnight but he knew if Martha Branigan ever found out there would be hell to pay. He decided it was none of his business; the girls confided in him about most things; when they were ready, one or the other of them would let him know what had been going on.

It had been a good many years since he had moved into Sea View; if he had known he was going to be there all this time he would have made more of an effort to make friends with some of the other residents. The trouble was, apart from Robert, they would all have been short-term friendships. Not a month seemed to go by without Mary or Pearl asking him if he would like to contribute to somebody or other's funeral flowers.

"The amount of money I have contributed since I've been here, I could open up my own florists!" he had remarked on the last occasion. "I hope when I go there will be enough of them left to donate to mine."

"Don't worry, Tom," Mary had replied. "If there's not, Pearl and I will buy you some ourselves."

By and large Tom had led a happy life, certainly a long one. He had often thought maybe it had been too long. Everyone else in the home was considerably younger than him these days, even the ones in their 70s were young enough to be his children. He missed so many things that when he was younger he'd taken for granted. For a start, he missed talking about things that both parties to the conversation could remember.

He missed all his old pals – Charlie, Dave, Jack, Ann, Jean and Jane – he could go on forever remembering all their names, but they were all gone now. He missed the simple things like a kiss on the cheek when friends met, or the occasional cuddle. Yes, above all, Tom missed a cuddle. At his time of life sex was but a distant memory but to have someone put their arms around you and just hold you, Tom missed that more than anything. Tom could still remember as if it were yesterday the last time Jenny cuddled him. His beloved Jenny, he missed her now more than ever. Everyone had told him that time was a great healer, that one day the pain of losing her would go away. Well it was not. The pain was as deep and hurtful now as it had been on the day she died. He remembered it as if it were yesterday.

As they lay there in bed together, having their usual banter, Jenny turned to Tom and said, "What would you do if anything happened to me and you were left on your own?"

Tom laughed. "Well, I would get up, have a shower, cook myself some breakfast and then go out and look for a younger model," he replied jokingly.

"You may laugh, Tom Hall, but I worry about these things. Anyway, you should be so lucky, you get out of breath cleaning your teeth – the sight of a naked young woman would kill you."

"Let me dream, girl, let me dream. It's a proven fact that women outlive their spouses by a good ten years, and as I am in no hurry to go anywhere just yet, you have nothing to worry about."

"Be serious Tom, I know I moan about you sometimes but you are the only man I have ever loved. If anything should happen to you and I was left on my own, I don't believe I could go on living."

"You are serious, girl, what brought this on?" Tom was beginning to feel concerned.

Jenny hesitated. "Well, for a start, I've been having some nasty dreams lately. Most of them have been about my mum and dad, they keep telling me it was time I came home. I also get this funny feeling every time you leave me on my own."

Tom looked at Jenny. "You should have told me before. I'll never leave you alone again." He put his arms round Jenny and hugged her to him.

She gazed up into his eyes and said, "Just promise me you will never leave me, Tom. I know you were only joking when you said most men die before their wives, but deep down something tells me that you won't. I don't know why, it's a feeling that's been niggling away in my mind for weeks now, and what with the dreams it frightens me. So promise me…" Jenny's eyes misted over as she snuggled into his strong and sturdy frame. Despite his age she still felt safe in his arms. She heard herself saying, "I will tell you when it's time for you to go, Thomas Hall, you will only go when I send for you."

Jenny lay back and closed her eyes, feeling the warmth of Tom's body and the beat of his heart; it was strong and steady. She loved him with all her being, no matter what he had done to hurt her in the past. She forgave him for everything. Surely no other feeling in this world or the next would be surpassed.

A voice was calling her, it was time to go home. As she felt Tom's arms tighten round her she was no longer afraid.

Tom stayed there for over an hour cradling Jenny in his arms, rocking gently backwards and forwards. He should have called an ambulance. How many times in the following weeks and months had he told himself, you bloody fool, you should have called an ambulance. But he had known instinctively that it was too late. Jenny had gone and he had kept his promise and been by her side until the end. He hugged her tightly to him and kissed her cheeks; he felt his body begin to shake, gently at first and then in deep heavy painful throbbing bursts. As the tears rolled down his cheeks onto Jenny's hair, Tom cried for the first time since he was a small boy.

It had been the children who'd taken control when Tom eventually gathered himself together and called them. His two sons Michael and Anthony had dropped everything and rushed to his side. Not young men themselves and with family responsibilities, they had made all the funeral arrangements and dealt with everything. Which was just as well as Tom was still in a complete daze.

The coroner explained to Tom that Jenny had died of an aneurysm on February 24th at 8.15 a.m. 2018 at the age of 82. Why the coroner thought he wanted to know how old Jenny was and when she had died was a mystery to him. He had been there, for Christ's sake.

Trying to put on a brave face, Tom had struggled along on his own for a while, but he was completely lost without Jenny, especially during the night. The nights were never ending, as he lay there lost and alone. What would he have given to feel Jenny by his side once again? All the little arguments and irritations that came between them as they aged paled into insignificance when the finality of Jenny's death hit him. Eventually, after a lot of soul searching, and a good many mishaps about the house, especially that fucking washing machine, Tom decided to put himself into a retirement home. At first the boys had been dead set against it, and did their best to persuade him to move in with one of them, but they were no longer spring chickens themselves and after realising their father had no intention of backing down, they had agreed. So Tom, with their help, drew up a contract with the Sea View retirement home and prepared to move in.

Albert Skinner paced up and down the corridor in the maternity unit of Eastbourne General Hospital. He had been pacing up and down now for nearly two hours. What was the delay? The midwife had told him that his lovely wife Ethel was about to have their first child any minute. That was two hours ago, what was holding things up? The question kept going through his mind. They had waited so long for this moment. He would die if anything went wrong now. Just as this thought crossed his mind, the doors of the maternity ward opened and a smiling black face appeared.

"Congratulations, Mr Skinner," Joyce Bakewell beamed in delight. In her arms she held a tiny bundle. "Say hello to your little baby girl. I shall always remember this little one. She shares her birthday with my own daughter."

Mary Jennifer Skinner. Born 24th February 2018, at 8.17 a.m. in the county of East Sussex, England.

9

Dr David

Dr David Cohen was the son of Rebecca and Samuel Cohen MD, a reasonably successful middle-class Jewish couple with, apart from their north London home, where David had been brought up, a second property in the South of France. They also owned a small motor launch berthed on the River Thames. David had had an extremely happy childhood within a very loving, if somewhat strict household. His parents insisted that he attended the local synagogue each week and observed all the Jewish holy days.

Indeed the proudest moment of their lives had been David's bar mitzvah where, according to the Jewish faith he had become a man. It was also David's proudest moment because anything that made his parents happy, made him happy.

Rebecca and Samuel had given him an expensive private education and sent him off to Leeds University to study medicine, where, having obtained his medical degree with honours, David decided, after spending a few years, first as a junior and later as a consultant in Leeds General Hospital, to give up the hectic lifestyle that comes with working in such a high pressure environment and become a general practitioner. He eventually found what he was looking for in the South of England in the seaside town of Eastbourne where he bought into a rather run down practice. First as a junior within the practice, then eventually progressing to become its senior partner. The area covered by the practice included the Sea View retirement home.

David had never married, not that he did not find the opposite sex attractive; his years at university had not been spent exclusively on furthering his education. But after years of his mother Rebecca trying to marry him off to every plump homely Jewish girl that ever visited their house, he had decided that life would prove to be much quieter if he remained single. At 45 years of age he had become set in his ways, quite content to see out his working life as a GP until he could retire to his parents' place in the South of France. After all, they wouldn't live forever. One day he would inherit it, along with the rest of their estate. Unfortunately for David, however, fate had a habit of turning a person's life upside down when they least expected it, and David's life was to be no exception.

Morning surgery over, David was looking forward to a stroll along the promenade before lunching at his favourite restaurant opposite the pier, followed by the usual nine holes of golf at Hampden Park, before returning for the evening surgery. The phone ringing in reception disturbed his thoughts but he chose to ignore it; after all, it was his receptionist's job to answer the bloody thing – that's what he paid her for. However, as he reached for his copy of The Times, David hoped it was not an emergency, or anything else that would spoil his plans for the afternoon.

Barely had David had time to open the paper before he was interrupted by Janet the receptionist tapping on the surgery door and entering. "Doctor, you're wanted on the phone, it's personal."

Trying not to let his irritation show too much David followed her into the reception and picked up the phone. "Yes?"

The sombre voice on the other end of the line enquired, "Is that you, David?" It was Rabbi Isaacs from his parents' synagogue.

During the drive up to London David's mind gradually began to grasp the sequence of events that had led to him being in heavy traffic, instead of playing golf in Hampden Park. Rabbi Isaacs had garbled something about a fire aboard the boat on the Thames, and his parents being rushed into hospital.

Thank God for car phones; never again would he say they intruded on his leisure time. Whilst on his way he had been able to arrange cover for the evening surgery as well as the following morning, if the need arose. The phone also enabled him to keep in touch with Rabbi Isaacs, who by all accounts was already at the hospital. This turned out to be a mixed blessing. Because before he could reach London he was informed his father had died. Finally, when he did reach his destination, it was only to find out his mother had passed away five minutes prior to his arrival.

From that moment on, things seemed to go from bad to worse. Even two months further down the line he could not believe how much his life had changed. Not physically, but inside, deep down in his soul. He no longer knew who he was; everything he had been brought up to believe in had been shattered.

It was his parents' solicitor who had dealt the final blow. Yes, OK, David was the main benefactor of their estate, but why had they left a considerable amount of money, some £50,000, to a Sarah Sheridan and why had they left a further £50,000 to an adoption society? He could understand certain other bequests to the various Jewish charities Rebecca had always been involved in. But why these two in particular? Well, he soon found out.

Back in north London for the second time within the space of a month, David stood outside the office of his parents' legal representative. Richard Newman and Partners, solicitors. Well, at least it was a good old Jewish name, and the sign above the door was brand new, which was more than could be said for the property itself. If ever there was a building due for demolition this was it. As to why he should have been summoned back to London so soon after his parents' demise was beyond him. As far as David was concerned everything should be quite straightforward and could have been conducted through the post without dragging him away from his practice.

David rang the front door bell and waited. There was a slight feeling of unease as he heard footsteps from within.

"Richard Newman, Samuel and Rebecca's solicitor and executor, you must be David. We have met before but you wouldn't remember, you were too young at the time."

Ushering David into a small cramped office, Richard removed a pile of papers from one of the leather chairs and offered him a seat.

"Sit down, David, can I get you a coffee or something?" David declined – he was anxious to get on. As he sat down and looked at the man sitting opposite him, he realised that the solicitor was older than he looked, around his parents' age, he guessed.

"What I am about to say to you, David, may come as a bit of a shock. I have known your parents since before you were born, and during all that time I have tried to persuade them to inform you of your background."

David felt distinctly uneasy. What background? He knew his background. He was the product of a good and loving Jewish couple.

Richard continued. "I was never very successful in my endeavours, and now at this unfortunate time in your life it has fallen upon my shoulders to explain the position to you. It will, I am sure, come as a great shock to learn that Samuel and Rebecca adopted you when you were only six weeks old, some years after discovering that Rebecca was unable to have children of her own.

David was stunned. How could this be? He possessed Rebecca's slightly ginger hair colouring and her easy manner. Everyone had said, even when he was a child, how like Samuel he was, with the same clear blue eyes. Now this bloody solicitor was telling him that he was an adopted child. Struggling to gather his senses, David was lost for words.

"Are you sure?" he stammered feebly. "Surely there must be some mistake?"

"I'm afraid I am sure, David, and there is defiantly no mistake. You see, all those years ago I was the person that Samuel and Rebecca turned to for help with the adoption process. I had hoped they would have plucked up the courage to tell you themselves, and I am sure they would have eventually but for their untimely demise. They loved you so much and as the years went by it got harder for them because they were frightened of losing you."

"They would never have lost me," David said quietly, "all I am or will ever be I owe to them."

"That would have made them very happy, David, but fear can make people behave in ways that otherwise they might not. They thought you would want to know about your birth mother and father, and I don't think they could risk that."

David pondered a minute. "Maybe I would have," he replied, "but I would never have stopped loving them; in fact I love them even more now that you have told me the truth. At least they wanted me, which is more than can be said for my birth parents."

"You don't know that, David. I am sure they loved you very much. More than you will ever know, because they had the courage to give you away."

"Who were they?" asked David, now beginning to sense that this man knew more than he was letting on.

For a moment the solicitor paused. Turning round, he rummaged through his filing cabinet and withdrew a battered file. "This is not an official record," he said, "it's something I kept in the event of you asking such a question. Your natural mother came from Ireland; we assume that your father was also Irish. I think your mother, I mean Rebecca, knew more than she let on, hence the large amount of money left in their will to a Sarah Sheridan, who incidentally I have had no luck in tracing. The money will remain with me until I succeed. If not, after seven years it will be yours.

David did not remember the return journey to Eastbourne; in fact he didn't remember much of the next few days. It was only when he decided to try and trace his natural mother, if she was still alive, that he began to think straight. The whole situation, despite the shock to his system, had its funny side. After all the years of following the Jewish faith and keeping up its traditions, it was more than possible that he wasn't even Jewish. If his biological parents came from Ireland it was odds on he was a bloody Catholic.

    David could not help smiling as he said to himself, I bet I'm the only Catholic boy in the land who has celebrated his very own bar mitzvah.

10

Jenny

Tom was not sure what made him choose the building industry as a career; he kind of drifted into it after trying his hand at various other methods of earning a living. Maybe it had been the freedom that the outdoor life offered him, or the sense of achievement that comes with giving something past its sell-by date a new lease of life. Throughout the years he certainly never lost the sense of fulfilment he got every time a job was completed to a client's satisfaction. Not many people could claim that after having spent nearly 60 years in the trade.

He felt sure he wouldn't be living in such comfortable surroundings if he had opted for a different path in life. Not that there had been much choice really, coming from a poor working class background meant that a university education was a no-no from the start. Despite the fact that Tom was quite bright at school and had been encouraged to go on to higher education, his mother had insisted that he left at 15 and start contributing to the family purse.

In spite of the earlier set-backs in life, everything had worked out for the best. If he hadn't decided to enter the building trade he would never have met Charlie King, which in turn meant never having met Jenny. That alone had made life worthwhile. Tom felt the tears beginning to well up inside as he recalled the events that led to their first meeting.

William James Ryland Ltd, was, apart from Tom Hall and Charlie King, staffed by what the two lads thought was a bunch of old codgers. Little did the two lads realise at the time how lucky they were having access to the skill and knowledge of so many artisans. Maybe it was this lack of appreciation in the face of such experience that drew them together as friends, creating an oasis of youth surrounded by the geriatric sands of time.

Work over for the day, Tom prepared to make his way home. Life at the moment was rather uneventful. He had recently ended his relationship with Audrey, the girl who worked for Owens the chemist and didn't fancy going out on his own. Although it was stretching the truth a bit to say that Tom had stopped seeing Audrey. She had been the one to say it was over and she didn't want to see him anymore. Apparently he was boring. Always talking about the old farts at work and how they had taught him to set out a staircase or pitch a roof, whatever that meant. If he was boring, she hadn't room to complain, going on as she did with her talk of pills and potions for sore throats, skin rashes, constipation and sore arses. Talk about the pot calling the kettle black.

Tom almost knocked Charlie over as he dashed out the yard gates. It had just started to rain and he could see the bus coming in the distance and with any luck he could beat it to the bus stop.

"Steady on, Tom, where's the fire?" Charlie looked aggrieved as he struggled to keep his feet.

Tom grinned. "Sorry, mate, didn't want to wait half an hour for the next bus. By the way, Chas, there's a new club recently opened up in Streatham, do you fancy giving it the once over tonight?"

Charlie shrugged his shoulders. He was at a loose end, a night out with Tom might be just the thing. "Why not? If it's no good we can always pop over to the ice rink across the road and eye up the girls in their short skirts. That blond bit from the paper shop said she was going there tonight and I said I might meet her there, but I don't want to appear too keen, in case she gets the wrong idea."

Tom and Charlie arranged to meet outside the main entrance of the club later that evening and Tom made his way home.

After a bite to eat, a quick shower and a change of clothes Tom was ready to make his way over to Streatham. With fortune on their side he and Charlie might strike it lucky and pick up a couple of birds, then that choosey cow Audrey could keep her free French letters; he would buy his own.

It hadn't stopped raining all evening as Tom waited for Charlie to appear and time was moving on. Now ten minutes to eight, there was still no sign of him. Where the bloody hell has he got to? If he doesn't turn up in the next ten minutes I'm off.

It was then that Tom saw her. Walking towards him was one of the most beautiful girls he had seen for ages. He remembered thinking, I wonder who the lucky guy is, as she approached.

Umbrella held high to ward off the rain, she nearly poked Tom's eye out as she stopped in front of him. "Tom Hall?"

Tom peered at her under her brolly. He felt his pulse begin to race as his mouth gaped open at the thought of her stopping to talk to him, let alone knowing his name.

"Shut your mouth, it makes you look stupid. Are you Tom Hall?"

Tom closed his mouth and nodded.

"Well I'm Charlie's sister. The idiot's slipped over in the bathroom and cut his head open, he won't be coming."

"Oh, how did that happen?" said Tom, momentarily at a loss for something to say. He couldn't have cared less how it happened. If the silly sod was unable to stand on his own two feet in the shower, what chance had he got on the dance floor? What Tom was more interested in was the vision of loveliness speaking to him at this moment.

65

"How the hell should I know, we don't share the same bath," she replied. "He was probably playing with himself as usual."

Tom sniggered to himself – something to goad his friend about when he next saw him. Pushing these thoughts to one side he plucked up enough courage to speak. "I suppose you wouldn't want to join me inside to see what's going on?" he enquired hopefully.

Jenny was about to say "You suppose right, dickhead" when she looked at Tom more closely. He was not a bad looking boy – quite well built, average height, and with lovely dark brown eyes that gave her a nice warm feeling inside. He was a little on the young side, probably never been out with a girl in his life. "How old are you, Tom?"

"Eighteen."

"OK then, you can be my toy boy. By the way, my name is Jennifer, but you can call me Jenny."

The two of them had a great night. Despite Jenny being two years Tom's senior they got on extremely well, and Tom was surprised at the end of the evening on their way home that it was Jenny who suggested maybe they should meet up again sometime. "Sure thing," he had replied, hoping that he didn't sound too eager.

Outside Jenny's house Tom bent over and kissed her gently on her lips. He was pleasantly aware of the closeness of her as he felt her respond. Thinking this was a signal to try his luck a little more, he moved his hand up from her waist to just under her breasts. Jenny stiffened and drew herself away from him. "That's your lot, big boy, I'll get Charlie to let you know when I'm free. Goodnight." With that she opened her front door and disappeared inside.

Once she was safely indoors, Jenny leaned against the back of the front door and let out a huge sigh of relief. That first kiss from Tom had unnerved her slightly. For a young lad he certainly knew how to press all the right buttons. It had taken her a great deal of willpower not to invite him in to spend the rest of the evening with her. All the other boys Jenny had courted in the past had been older than her; Tom was the first to be younger, an experience Jenny was keen to repeat.

All the way home Tom could not believe his good fortune – a girl like Jenny fancying him. He could not wait for the next time they went out together.

The following morning as he approached the gates of the builders' yard he spotted Charlie coming towards him from the opposite direction, hands in his pockets and whistling away to himself. Tom thought he couldn't have injured himself too much otherwise he would not be coming into work. He paused at the gates and waited for Charlie to catch up. "Morning, mate, how's the head?"

Charlie looked a bit sheepish. "Not too bad. I slipped on the soap as I was getting out of the shower. I'm sorry about last night by the way. But Jenny told me you had a great time without me anyway."

Tom laughed. "Yes we did actually. Your sister's a terrific bird isn't she? Oh and by the way, Charlie, she told me it was not slipping on the soap that made you cut your head open, but we won't go into that too much." Tom was sure Charlie turned pink around the gills, but thought maybe he should let the matter drop; he could not afford to upset him in case it affected any future relationship with his sister.

Just as this thought crossed his mind, Charlie raised the subject himself. "Yes, for some reason my sister was quite impressed by you. Normally she goes for the older guy. Unless of course she has taken up cradle snatching? Tell me, Tom, what's your secret?"

It was now Tom's turn to go pink around the gills. "I don't know what you're talking about," he stammered. "We just seemed to hit it off, that's all."

"Well you must have got something right because she wants to know if you would like to see her again tonight."

Tom could hardly conceal his excitement. "Yeah, great," he replied. "What time and where?"

"Come round to my place when you've had your tea, about eight I should think. I'm off to the pictures with that bird from the paper shop, so I won't be there."

The yard gates swung open and a head appeared. "Are you two lazy buggers going to stand there all day jawing or are you going to do some work?"

Oh what a long day, it was! Bad enough pulling down ceilings at the best of times, but today of all days when he had a date with Jenny. The dust and dirt got up his nose and down his throat; in fact it penetrated every orifice of his body. It was no good thinking about a shower tonight. He would have to spend at least half an hour soaking in a hot bath to get properly clean. If he turned up at Jenny's place with grimy fingernails or dirt in his ears he would die of shame. Even worse if he got lucky and she found ceiling plaster among his more private places.

Finally five o'clock arrived and Tom was off. As he dashed away from the yard, he wondered how and where he and Jenny would spend the evening. They could go and see a film of course, but there was always a possibility they would bump into Charlie with that stupid bird from the paper shop. That was the last thing Tom wanted. Charlie seemed to like his women to be a bit simple. Meeting up with them would be like taking Jenny on a kid's outing. Maybe they could go back to the club in Streatham; he would let her decide.

*

Tom almost knocked Charlie off his feet for the second time that week as he rushed past him on the way to the bus stop.

With the sound of Charlie's curses ringing in his ears Tom turned to wave his apologies, only to narrowly avoid running under the wheels of a passing lorry.

"Watch it you stupid bastard! I don't want to have to tell my sister her toy boy has ended up in the mortuary."

Arriving at Jenny's house dead on eight o'clock as Charlie had suggested, Tom couldn't help noticing his hand shaking as he rang the front door bell. After what seemed to be ages, the door opened and a quite smart middle-aged woman greeted him. "You must be Tom. Jenny won't be a minute, she's just finishing getting ready." Indicating that he should come in, she led him into a comfortably furnished lounge and told to him to take a seat. "I'm Jenny's mum by the way, you can call me Barbara. I have to leave you now, I'm meeting my husband from work. We're going to the theatre. Have a nice evening." With that she left the room and Tom heard the front door close behind her as she left the house.

Tom sat there alone, nervously glancing around the room. It was nicely decorated and well furnished, unlike his own home, which was poor by comparison. He was about to get up from his seat and have a closer look at some photographs on the mantelpiece when the door opened and Jenny appeared. "Sorry I'm not ready, Tom, but I was late in from work and I'm shattered." She was still in her dressing gown and had a towel wrapped round her head. "Unless you are really keen to go out, I wouldn't mind staying in and watching television or play some music."

Tom didn't mind at all, he couldn't think of anything he would like more than to spend the evening alone with a girl like Jenny. "That's fine by me," he replied, hoping he wasn't sounding too eager. "I've had a hard day myself, so it will be nice to stay in and relax."

Jenny picked up a pile of records from the top of the Dansette record player and handed them to Tom. "Here, you choose." Plonking herself down on the sofa, she drew her legs up behind her and motioned Tom to come and join her. Together they sat browsing through a mixture of 78 and 45 records, but all Tom could think about was the warmth of Jenny's body through her dressing gown. He could hear Jenny chatting away but precisely what she was saying escaped him. His mind was on other things.

"It's obvious you are not too keen on watching the television or listening to any of my music," Jenny said, as she took the records from him and placing them on the floor beside her. "You haven't heard a word I've been saying." She lent over and kissed him gently on the lips. "I hope you are not too tired after your busy day," she whispered.

Tom could feel her hand resting on his inner thigh. His mind was about to explode; never in his wildest dreams did he think a girl like Jenny would fancy him, let alone make the first move. He felt himself swell with anticipation as he attempted to embrace her, but his over anxious advances only caused them to overbalance and topple off the sofa onto the floor.

They lay there side-by-side, giggling like two naughty children, exploring each other with their hands, enjoying the warmth and closeness of their bodies as they touched. Somehow it seemed the most natural thing in the world that they should be there together.

Tom could not contain himself any longer. As he unzipped his jeans to remove them, he felt Jenny's restraining hand. "Not here, let's go upstairs," she whispered," leading him by the hand up to her bedroom. "It's better to be up here in case Charlie comes back," she explained simply before untying her dressing gown and letting it fall to the floor.

Never before had Tom seen such beauty. Even in magazines or films, nothing could compare with the girl that stood before him.

"Go and take a shower," she whispered, "and here, put this on." Scooping up her dressing gown she held it out towards him.

Tom had had some quick showers in his time, but this one must have broken all records. He was still dripping wet as he made his way to Jenny's room. She was lying on the bed with a pink duvet clasped tightly up round her neck staring at the ceiling. As Tom entered the room, Jenny lifted the duvet cover and patted the bed beside her, indicating for him to join her. She giggled as she felt his wet body come into contact with her own.

Together they made love, gently and unhurried, Jenny pleasantly surprised that this young boy should show such patience and consideration for her needs. So unlike the wham-bam technique she had experienced from so-called more mature lovers.

They made love throughout the night, pausing only to listen as Charlie came home and went to his room, and again when Jenny's parents returned from their evening at the theatre, until they fell asleep, exhausted but happy in each other's arms.

Earlier that evening when Jenny had removed her bathrobe and Tom had seen her naked for the first time, he had noticed a small birthmark in the shape of a lopsided chevron high up on her inner thigh. When he remarked upon it Jenny had laughed and said her father always told her when she was a little girl that it was a sign from God indicating that she was perfect, and that it was his tick of approval. Tom could not have agreed more.

As the early hours of the morning approached, Jenny turned over to find Tom with his back towards her, still fast asleep; he looked so fresh faced and innocent lying there. She leant over and kissed him on the cheek. Sliding her hand down his back she felt her way until she found what she was looking for. Her gentle caress stirred him into life and Jenny felt him harden. "Once more, Tom, then you must leave before anyone finds out you're here."

Tom quietly closed the door behind him and crept up to the front gate. Glancing back, he saw Jenny waving to him as he strode onto the street and into the morning air.

He felt 10 ft tall, his brisk walk turned into a run as he made his way home. For the first time he noticed the dawn and how beautiful it was. The birds were singing at him from the rooftops of the houses as he dashed by. Normally so drab, they now looked like little palaces. For the first time Tom realised he was in love.

11

The Newcomer

Mary Skinner loved working at Sea View. For a start she considered herself extremely fortunate to have secured a job there in the first place and was determined to prove that in choosing her, Miss Branigan had made the right choice. Certainly all the other applicants had been far more experienced than Mary, and possessed a lot more confidence. Pearl, being the eternal sceptic that she was, said Mary's success was probably down to the fact that Martha Branigan liked to impose her standards on all the staff and stood more chance of doing so with someone lacking experience than she did with other more mature candidates.

But the icing on the cake for her had been when Martha suggested that she move into the vacant bedsit in the annexe. Even in Eastbourne, if you were lucky enough to find a flat for rent it would cost the earth. So the added bonus of free accommodation was not to be sneezed at. It would allow her to save until she could afford a place of her own. Once again Pearl thought this was probably because if Mary moved into the annexe she would be on call night and day. Just like she was. "That woman doesn't do anything for nothing. You mark my words, sooner or later she will want something in return."

Yes, Mary thought, it had certainly been a stroke of luck the day she decided to apply for the post of junior nurse at

Sea View, and now Martha trusted her enough to be left in charge, as well as being given the responsibility of attending to the new arrival.

With Pearl away on one of her rare days off, apparently up in London with Malcolm, and Martha Branigan having to attend a meeting about Tom's forthcoming birthday celebrations, Mary had been thrilled that Martha trusted her enough to deal with the newcomer. Well, at least this one was a man. Any more women and poor old Tom would have to consider wearing a dress so as to blend in with his surroundings.

Mr Floyd Bakewell, Mary thought, was a man in his late 60s or early 70s and of Caribbean origin. It was obvious just by looking at him that Floyd had recently suffered a stroke and found it difficult to move around freely. He also had a sad look in his eyes, like a man who had been badly let down.

Sea View in some ways was like the 'bush telegraph'. Mary never ceased to be amazed how days, if not weeks before a new arrival appeared, everybody in the home knew all about them. The current rumour about Floyd was that when he became ill, his partner had left him to fend for himself and ran off with somebody else. Whatever the truth, and Mary suspected that probably only half of what she had heard was fact, Floyd would make a good companion for Tom, because when she had helped him unpack she had noticed a chess set among his belongings. It had been a long time since Tom had enjoyed a game, not since Robert died in fact. Come to think of it Floyd's surname was the same as Pearl's; maybe he would turn out to be a distant relative. One thing was for sure, Floyd Bakewell would be the topic of conversation for the next few weeks until the novelty of his arrival wore off, or somebody else arrived to divert their attention.

Mary liked Pearl; despite their age difference they had 'hit it off' straight away. The fact that they celebrated their birthday on the same day seemed to have given them a special bond.

Pearl had always wanted a career in a caring profession; strange how her mother dealt with those that came into this world while she concentrated all her efforts on those about to leave it. Perhaps, as Pearl's mother had said, we all need a little help at some time or other, whether starting life or ending it, although perhaps not with the same enthusiasm.

For as long as she could remember there had been something inside Mary guiding her towards her ambition to be a nurse. Her dolls were her first patients, to be loved and looked after until she grew too old to play with them anymore. That is, all except for the teddy bear, Mary would never be too old for the teddy bear. Even to this day she still kept him in the place of honour, tucked up in her bed.

Mary remembered as if it was yesterday the day that her father brought him home.

Albert Skinner was pleased with himself; he had won one of the minor prizes in the firm's annual spring raffle and was on his way to present it to his beautiful daughter.

Mary was to be three years old in the morning and it would make a nice surprise present for her, along with the other one hundred and one things Ethel had bought. Albert wrapped his prize in shiny gold paper and attached a heart-shaped card to it on which he wrote *'Please look after me, I'm lost'*. Placing his trophy on a chair at the kitchen table he waited for Mary to arrive home from nursery school.

Mary was beside herself with excitement; her mother had met her at the nursery school gates and told her that Daddy had a surprise for her when she got home. What could it be? Hopefully not another doll or anything to do with school, or worse still, clothes. No, Mary was sure that if her daddy bought her a present it would be something wonderful.

Albert could see the excitement in his daughter's eyes turn to disappointment as he handed her the package. Maybe she thought it was just another doll, it was the same shape. He watched anxiously as Mary slowly removed the wrapping to expose a furry brown leg. Immediately her attitude changed and tearing at the gold paper she removed her present and clasped it tightly to her chest. Her eyes were dancing with delight. "Where have you been? I've waited for you for such a long time; I thought you would never come. Tommy, you are mine, all mine." Albert and Ethel looked at one another in amazement. Well, at least the present was a resounding success, and by the sound of it the teddy bear had already been given a name.

Funny how after all these years Mary's favourite resident should be called Tom? It wasn't that Mary didn't get on with all of the other residents at Sea View; it was just that right from day one she and Tom had formed a close bond. Maybe it was because he stood out from all the others due to his great age, or perhaps it was that he reminded her of her teddy bear, so warm and cuddly with the same sparkling big brown eyes. Whatever the reason, Mary sensed it was something special.

The one thing that Mary didn't like about Sea View, however, was the deaths. Just as you got to know and like a person and became used to their idiosyncrasies they would pop off and you had to start the process with somebody new all over again. Pearl told her that she must learn to deal with people coming and going because that was what the home was all about, and that she wasn't to let it upset her.

But it did, and Mary hated it when one of her flock died.

Martha Branigan, on the other hand, was as hard as nails. She had never shown any emotion whatsoever; to her the death of a resident was a minor inconvenience, causing her extra paperwork If they died they died. It meant finding a replacement to keep the finances of the home in good order, which in turn meant more work for her, but apart from that the business of running Sea View went on. If, however, like Tom Hall they appeared to live forever, so that they almost became part of the furniture, so much the better; at least those ones provided a steady income.

Eventually it had been Tom who noticed how upset Mary became each time a resident died and tried to put things in perspective by giving her the benefit of his experience and wisdom.

"Whenever I have lost someone, Mary, I find it helps if you try to imagine that they are only in the next room, or that they have just popped out for a while. That way you gradually get used to them not being there. One day if you are as lucky as I was, you will meet someone and fall in love. When that day comes, make the most of it and treasure every moment, because before you know it the years will have flown past. Should Lady Luck smile on you and allow you to grow old together, there will come a time when it will dawn on you that eventually one of you must die and the other will be left alone.

"You will agonise over whether you would want to go first so that you never feel the pain and loneliness of losing the most precious person in your life, or hope that the one you love dies before you to prevent them having to suffer. I am afraid that for people who truly love one another it is the price they have to pay. Deep down I am thankful my Jenny was spared the agony and loneliness that I have endured these past 20 years. That is the price we each have to pay for the precious gift of love. Anyway, let's not be so morbid, everyone living here has led a long and healthy existence otherwise they would not be here in the first place. So save your tears for those who die young and never make it into old age."

Mary bent over and kissed Tom on the forehead before dashing out of the room in case he should see her tears.

12

Fiona

Fiona Philips was upstairs at the front of the house looking out of her bedroom window. She had just got out of the bath and was still in her dressing gown.

The street below was deserted apart from the mongrel dog from three doors away cocking his leg up the side of a brand new car belonging to the woman across the road. Serve her right for parking it right opposite our drive, thought Fiona. With the whole of the road to choose from, as well as having a driveway of her own, the bloody woman chose to park it there right on the bend opposite her house. Fiona made a mental note to save the bone from next Sunday's roast for the dog and proceeded to survey the empty street.

For a summer's day, it didn't seem very much like summer. It had started to rain just after 7 a.m. that morning and now it was pissing down. Her husband had left the house at 6.30 to play his weekly round of golf and she was bored. Perhaps if they had children of their own she wouldn't find life so boring, but Peter was adamant that he was too old to start a family now. Selfish bastard. If Peter spent as much time with her as he did playing golf, maybe she wouldn't be feeling so neglected. Why should she have to make do with looking after her sister's kids every once in a while?

Why he had insisted on playing golf in such weather was beyond her. But this wasn't the first time; he had often gone off to play in the pouring rain, but always returned home bone dry. She had suspected for some time now that there was more to him playing golf than met the eye.

A sudden movement at the side entrance of the house caught her attention. The rain seemed to be easing off a little and signs of life were beginning to emerge. It was Tom. Despite the heavy downpour he was still working. Fiona was glad that Peter had decided to employ Tom Hall's company to carry out the contract work on their new extension. It had been a toss up between him and a larger building company in Streatham. When Peter had interviewed them each in turn, it was Tom Hall that she had preferred. He had been polite and reserved, while his opposition was brash and over confident with a lecherous look in his eye every time he spoke to her.

Fiona watched as Tom pushed the heavy wheelbarrow up the narrow plank on to his lorry before tipping its contents on to the growing heap of rubble. He was soaked to the skin, his tight fitting shirt clinging to his upper body, emphasising the muscles in his arms. His jeans were sticking to his legs, giving the impression that he was a ballet dancer performing some strange routine from Swan Lake, instead of loading rubbish onto the back of a lorry. She wondered what it would feel like to have those strong arms embrace her and to experience the closeness of his wet body pressed up against her own. Dragging herself away from the window Fiona scolded herself for having such thoughts; she must be at least four years Tom's senior, why should he show the remotest interest in her?

Fiona removed her dressing gown and stood back to admire her naked body in the mirror. It was not bad for a woman of her age; there were many of her friends that were years younger who could not boast of a figure as firm and shapely. She ran her hands over her breasts and down her abdomen, experiencing a pleasant tingle as her fingers glided gently over her body.

The sound of her name being called out made her jump; she grabbed her dressing gown and held it up against her upper body before venturing out on to the landing to see who was calling her. It was Tom; he was standing in the hallway looking up at her as she peered over the banisters. "I'm sorry to disturb you, Mrs Philips," he stuttered, "but do you mind if I use your downstairs cloakroom to change out of my wet clothes?"

Fiona was sure he was blushing; the back of his neck had turned quite red. "Go ahead, Tom," she replied, "I will be down in a minute to make you a hot drink."

As she retreated back into the bedroom Fiona caught a glimpse of herself in the mirror. She was still clutching the dressing gown to her upper body, the hem of which had somehow managed to get itself hooked up on to her engagement ring, leaving the bottom half of herself completely naked. Anyone standing downstairs in the hall would have had a bird's eye view of what she had to offer. No wonder Tom Hall had turned red around the gills.

Opening the wardrobe she grabbed the first dress that came to hand and slipped it over her naked form, anxious to get downstairs before Tom came out of the cloakroom. She passed the door on her way to the kitchen and called out to him to fetch his wet clothes so that she could put them in the dryer.

By the time Tom emerged, Fiona had already made the coffee. She turned to take the wet bundle from him and smiled. "I suppose in your job you get used to carrying a change of clothes with you."

"Well it helps," replied Tom, "but not everyone is as helpful as you, Mrs Philips."

Fiona laughed. "You don't have to call me Mrs Philips, Tom, we have known one another long enough by now. Call me Fiona."

She could see the back of Tom's neck begin to turn red, and smiled to herself. Was he remembering the view from the bottom of the stairs, she wondered? He had certainly seen a lot more of her than she had planned.

Tom walked over to the draining board and helped himself to one of the coffees. He noticed as Fiona bent over to put his wet clothes in the machine that she wasn't wearing anything under her dress and could feel himself getting hot under the collar. "Thank you, Mrs Philips… err, I mean Fiona."

Fiona switched on the dryer and went to pick up her coffee. Tom was still standing with his back resting on the sink unit sipping his own coffee as she squeezed past between him and the kitchen table. Their bodies touched, and as she reached for her drink, she could smell his body – a strange mixture of aftershave and body odour.

The strain of loading rubbish onto his lorry had made him sweat. What would have normally made her recoil in horror if it had been Peter, she now found to be exciting. In the brief time that their bodies were close, Fiona could feel that Tom was aroused; his hands were shaking and she could hear his cup rattling on its saucer. Placing her own drink on the kitchen table Fiona removed the offending crockery from his grasp and placed it down on the draining board beside him. Their closeness left her in no doubt as to his condition and it excited her. Not for a long time had she felt this way. Fiona could feel Tom responding as she began to gyrate her pelvis. She raised her head up to kiss him on the lips, her tongue thrusting deep into his mouth.

The sound of a key turning in the front door lock had the effect of an electric shock. Fiona and Tom jumped apart as if they had been poked with an electric cattle prod.

Normally Fiona would have heard the car pull into the drive. That alone usually gave her time to prepare for Peter's return. By the time he had put his clubs in the garage and cleaned his golf shoes, she would have made his coffee and put toast under the grill.

Peter entered the kitchen and placed his car keys on the table. "Coffee smells nice, darling, is there one left for me?" He smiled at Tom, who was standing facing the sink unit gazing out of the window, coffee cup in his hand. "Morning Tom, not a very nice day today, I suppose you have been rained off this morning?"

Tom nodded; he felt he should turn round to face Peter but was still quite excited from his encounter with Fiona. "Yes," he said, still looking intently out of the window, "I got absolutely soaked, but Mrs Philips was kind enough to dry my wet clothes for me."

"Tom," Fiona interrupted, "I have told you, call me Fiona and I am sure my husband won't mind if you call him Peter."

Peter nodded in agreement. "Of course, Tom, after all you have become more like a friend over the past few weeks." With that, Peter turned to Fiona. "I'll just put my clubs in the garage and clean my shoes, and I'll take my coffee with me."

So that's why she never heard him arrive home. He had broken with his routine. Fiona could always rely on the whine of the mechanism on the garage door; it told her that Peter would be busy for the next few minutes.

The pair of them breathed a huge sigh of relief. Tom had now resumed his former position with his back to the sink unit and was finishing his coffee. Fiona walked over to him and removed the empty cup from his shaking hand. Placing it to one side, she kissed him on the cheek. "I think you had better leave now, Tom," she said quietly. "Another time perhaps."

Tom nodded his agreement. At this moment in time he was lost for words, but there was disappointment in his eyes. As he prepared to leave Fiona placed her hands inside his open shirt and laid her head on his chest, the closeness of him rekindling her desire. She moved her fingers up and down Tom's spine, almost fainting as she felt that he was ready to burst. She pressed herself against him, unable to control her feelings any longer. Slowly Fiona sank to her knees, her face still firmly pressed against Tom's now perspiring torso. Her breath was now coming in short sharp bursts. In all the years she had been married to Peter, despite his pleas, Fiona had never consented to provide him with the service she was about to give to Tom. Quickly unfastening his waistband, she released his zip. Lowering her head she relieved him of all the tension of the day.

13

Robert

It wasn't really Tom's fault that everything had come to a head that morning. He and Robert were enjoying one of their rare games of chess while chatting away about old times when all of a sudden Robert had erupted. All Tom had done was to ask him a simple question.

Robert couldn't help remembering how he and Simon used to enjoy a game of chess. Ever since the onset of his ill health, Simon had been a keen player. He would sit there, just like Tom was now, pondering over his next move or chatting away about all the silly things that made them both laugh. It was at times like this that Robert missed his friend most.

Tom, as ever, was going on about Jenny and how he missed her even after all these years, gently probing with his questions about Robert's past, whether or not he had ever been married, or if he had any family. The more Tom prattled away the more Robert was reminded of Simon and how much it hurt without him. Suddenly Tom asked him a direct question, staring at him intently with those dark brown eyes of his. He enquired, " Do you miss your partner like I miss Jenny, Robert? What was she like? You never talk about her."

Robert's mind was in a whirl; he could avoid the subject no longer. He heard himself shouting in an almost hysterical voice,

"Him. I miss *him*. Just like you miss your Jenny, but I don't keep bloody well going on and on about it. Do you understand me? My partner was a he. His name was Simon. Yes I miss him every single day, as much if not more than you miss your bloody Jenny. Now will you stop asking me any more questions and leave me alone." With that Robert had got up and left the lounge as all eyes turned to follow his departure.

Tom sat there stunned, and completely deflated. The last thing he wanted was to upset Robert. Robert was his one true friend since moving into Sea View. He wished now that he had minded his own business and kept his mouth shut.

Tom decided to give Robert time to cool down before going to see how the land lay. He was conscious of Jack Holland sniggering in the background but decided not to comment; he had caused enough trouble for one day, upsetting another resident would only make matters worse. Tom made his way across the lounge on the way back to his room, unable to avoid passing the sneering Jack Holland's table. One word, just one word from you, thought Tom, and I'll shove this chessboard right up where the sun doesn't shine.

Robert was beside himself with remorse. Why had he verbally attacked Tom like that? It had been Tom that had befriended him when all the other residents chose to ignore him, Tom that had made the past 15 years more bearable. Without him as a companion life would have been very lonely indeed. Now he had ruined it all with his outburst. It had been a combination of his desire to share the secrets of his past, with the fear that if he did, he might lose Tom's friendship and respect.

He knew after all these years Tom still missed Jenny; had he not told him every other day for the last decade and a half? He also knew Tom was still lonely, despite their friendship. Well, so was he, but too proud to tell anyone.

Robert and Simon had been together for 40 years when Simon had his first stroke. Fit and healthy and full of fun, they had lived, loved and laughed together right up to that fateful day when he had woken up one morning unable to speak properly or get out of bed unaided. Even then Robert never realised the seriousness of Simon's illness. The slight loss of movement down one side quickly returned to normal after a few weeks of exercise, and the slur in his speech Simon made a joke of, assuring Robert that it was nothing to be concerned about. "Don't worry, all our friends will think that I'm just slightly pissed as usual," he laughed. After a couple of months of cutting down on the cigarettes and alcohol, Simon eventually became bored with the whole process and retuned to his gregarious ways.

Robert had been going out with some girl from the salon when he and Simon first met. What was her name … Patricia somebody or other? He had taken her to the Wimbledon Palais dance hall in South London, but within half an hour of them being there, she had spotted an old flame that she still fancied and dumped him there and then.

Not that it had concerned him much at the time; her departure could well turn out to be her loss and his gain. After all there was plenty of other 'talent' about. He sat there sipping his orange juice, lost in a world of his own, when all of a sudden the air was filled with wolf whistles and laughter. Looking up, Robert saw this strange figure in a pink suit and a bright yellow tie flouncing across the dance floor. Before he could distinguish whether it was male or female the pink and yellow apparition, complete with cigarette holder and shoulder bag, was at his table. "Hello sweetie, is this seat taken?" Robert laughed then and hadn't stopped laughing throughout all the years he and Simon were together. "Feel free" he had replied.

Plonking himself down, the pink apparition said, "Hi, I'm Simon."

Simon, as it turned out when Robert could get a word in edgeways, was a choreographer, dance was his life. He and Robert chatted away as if they had been friends for years, oblivious to all the giggles and funny looks of all those around them. They defied convention to become partners. And for the next 40 years or more, Robert was to support Simon throughout everything he attempted in life, accompanying him to his dance venues, helping to calm him down when things got too stressful and above all, by just being there.

To a great extent Robert had sacrificed his own career so that Simon could achieve his main ambition of becoming a top-flight dance teacher. It was a year or maybe 18 months after they first met that Robert decided to give up working in the salon. Their relationship had been going from strength to strength and Simon had broached the subject of Robert moving in with him.

Roberts's work as a high-class hairdresser was becoming more and more difficult, with all the petty rules and regulations being imposed upon him by the local authority, as well as the ever-increasing costs of hiring his chair, and recent events with the health and safety officer had been the last straw.

Simon's career, on the other hand, was blossoming. Not only had he been asked to choreograph a new West End show, he was also appearing on television as one of the judges in a popular dance programme.

All this, coupled with his regular work of teaching the next generation of 'wanabee' youngsters how to dance, meant they were spending less and less time together. The final decision, although taken at the end of one of their dinner parties, really stemmed from an earlier incident that had taken place that week, the story of which Robert related to their guests over dinner.

Robert did not own the hairdressing salon where he worked; he only rented a chair on the premises, paying a monthly rent for its use. This entitled him to have the use of all the salon's facilities and to maintain a list of his own clients, many of whom were titled ladies.

It was while he was styling the hair of a particularly fussy client, a certain Lady Rochmere, that he was interrupted by the health and safety officer for the third time that week. Not only was this officer in question very officious, he had obviously taken a dislike to Robert.

First he examined the chair as Robert struggled to keep his client calm, moving it first one way and then the other, much to the annoyance of its occupant. He then proceeded to tilt it up and down and backwards and forwards.

"Is this necessary while I am working?" asked Robert.

"Well, of course," was the reply. "I need to ensure it is safe and fit for purpose." The officer then moved over to the washbasin and examined the surrounding implements. Noticing a plastic container with various combs and scissors, he picked it up and peered into it. "Does this contain a suitable disinfectant?" he asked.

"Yes," replied Robert tersely.

"Have you got a separate washbasin to wash your hands, before attending to your clients?"

"Yes."

Lady Rochmere let out a sigh. "Do you think you could hurry along, Robert? There's a dear. I have an appointment."

Robert apologised profusely before turning to the health and safety officer. "You must excuse me, but as you can see, this lady is in a hurry and I would like to get on with my work. Maybe you could come back when we are closed to the public?"

Ignoring Robert completely, the health and safety officer turned to the array of equipment displayed beside the washbasin. He began to pick up each of the items in turn and examine them closely. "Are all these instruments regularly steamed cleaned and disinfected?"

"YES, YES," Robert said, beginning to lose his cool. "Are you sure all this is absolutely necessary?"

The officer looked up from his examination of the items in front of him. "Well of course, how else are we to protect the general public from all sorts of mishaps and infections? Things like head lice or septicaemia and many others besides, including AIDS."

At this point Robert completely lost his composure. His eyes began to bulge as his neck and face turned almost purple. "AIDS!" he screamed, "AIDS! Excuse me. What sort of establishment do you think we run? We don't fuck our clients here, we give them a haircut."

A deathly silence descended over the salon as heads turned towards Robert's chair; clients raised themselves from various stages of either having a shampoo or from being under the dryer to gaze in his direction.

The health officer turned as white as a ghost. Searching desperately for the nearest exit he muttered his apologies and beat a hasty retreat.

Robert, for his part, wished the floor would open and swallow him up. Never in the whole of his career had he lost his temper like that in front of his clients.

Turning to Lady Rochmere, he began to apologise profusely. She reached over and patted his hand. "Well said, Robert, well said. You were quite right about the service you provide, more's the pity."

Finishing her hair after what seemed an age, Robert once more apologised for his outburst, only to be reassured he had nothing to be sorry for. After all she had heard worse from her husband when he returned from the House of Lords. It was only after Lady Rochmere had left the salon that Robert realised she had trebled his usual tip.

As his dinner guests burst into laughter at the completion of Robert's story, Simon suggested that it might be better if Robert gave up working in the salon and joined him 'on the road'. The rest, as the saying goes, is history, although Robert did refuse to give up his hairdressing completely and retained some of his more wealthy or titled clients. Among them a certain Lady Rochmere who seemed to have developed a special bond with Robert since his outburst in the salon, insisting that now she no longer visited the 'shop', Simon and Robert must call her Helen.

Each month her ladyship would arrive at their house for her 'fix' as she liked to call it, in her battered old Ford Anglia, nearly demolishing the front hedge as she entered the drive and at the risk of life and limb to any passing pedestrian.

Stopping just in time to avoid reducing the garage to a pile of rubble, Lady Helen Rochmere would wave cheerfully to the two pale, almost ghostly faces peering at her from the window.

Robert fussed over his 'special' client, titivating what was left of Lady Helen's somewhat rapidly disappearing hair, after which Simon would prepare tea and cakes in the lounge and entertain her while Robert backed the battered Ford Anglia out of the drive onto the highway. This was Robert's way of doing his bit for humanity, in order to avoid any unsuspecting passer-by meeting an untimely end. But not before he had enquired which way Lady Helen would be travelling so that he could point her car in the right direction.

The relief when Lady Helen Rochmere's car disappeared from view showed on the faces of Simon and Robert as they closed their front door, comforted in the knowledge that all in the area were safe for at least another month.

Throughout all the years that Robert had spent with Simon, the only things that disturbed him were Simon's liking for the red wine and his incessant smoking. Time and time again he had begged Simon to cut down on his alcoholic intake and to give up smoking altogether. But no, Simon loved his 'fag'. His idea of heaven was to relax in the garden with a glass of red wine in one hand and that sodding ivory cigarette holder in the other, puffing away like the London to Brighton steam train. Robert had lost count of the times he had threatened to throw "that bloody thing" in the bin. "One day that thing will be the death of you," he had said on many occasions, and in the end he had been proved right.

The second stroke came out of the blue. Just as they thought Simon had gotten over the worst. Robert had taken Simon his usual early morning cup of tea and placed it at the right side of his bed so as to make it easier for him to reach. Five minutes later he had returned to pick up what he thought would be the empty cup, only to find it still full.

"Come on lazy bones," Robert said jokingly, "move that fat backside of yours."

There had been no reply.

After that everything proceeded at breakneck speed. He had called for an ambulance and Simon was rushed into hospital. Even at that stage Robert thought eventually everything would be fine; after all Simon had been a dancer all his life, you would have to go a long way to find somebody as fit and active as him at his age.

When he eventually did come home, despite extensive therapy Simon was confined to bed; he had lost most of his power of speech and the use of his arms and legs. As Robert sat there reflecting on the past, he found himself wondering why on earth he had stood at Simon's bedside holding that blasted cigarette holder for him so that he could enjoy a smoke. Maybe it was because despite the disapproval of what Robert thought was a disgusting habit, it was one of Simon's little pleasures. God knows, towards the end they were few and far between; even a glass of wine had to be sipped through a straw. At least that last cigarette of an evening restored a little bit of Simon's dignity.

Three weeks after coming out of hospital Simon died peacefully in his sleep. Robert sighed; well at least Simon had been grateful, the letter proved that.

A gentle tap on his door disturbed Roberts's thoughts. As he opened it he saw Tom's face grinning at him sheepishly. "Fancy a walk down the front?"

14

The Garage Door

Over a month had gone by now since the episode in the kitchen at the Philips' house, so Tom felt that at last he could now relax. There had been no repercussions to date and with the work on their extension finally completed the chances of him meeting up with Fiona again were remote.

The first week had been the worst; as hard as Tom tried to obliterate the incident from his mind, the harder it became. The memory of Fiona's body close to his and the ensuing service would return when he least expected it to, and then the process of trying to forget her would have to start all over again. Tom also knew that Jenny suspected there was something not quite right between them. When she had asked what was troubling him, his denial only seemed to make her even more suspicious. The mental strain he had put himself under was beginning to affect him in ways that were hard to disguise, the main one being when he and Jenny attempted to make love. Despite all these problems, however, Tom felt sure he could now forget what had happened and vowed nothing like it would ever happen again.

What a tiring day it had been. Moving 6 m of ready-mix concrete down a passageway too narrow to take a wheelbarrow was hard work. Tom's arms were red raw through carrying the heavy metal buckets filled with concrete. He couldn't wait to get home and have a hot bath to relieve his aches and pains. As he entered the front door, Jenny called out to him from the kitchen. "A Mr Peter Philips called today; he wants you to give him a ring, he sounded quite anxious to speak to you." Tom's heart missed a beat. Was his cosy world about to be blown apart? He was sure that Fiona, unable to live with the guilt of what had happened in her kitchen, had confessed all to Peter. How would he explain to Jenny, that in a moment of madness he had risked all for two minutes of pleasure. Certain that he was about to be confronted, Tom decided to delay making the call for as long as possible. His mind was working overtime. He couldn't place the entire blame for what had happened on Fiona; after all he had been more than a willing partner.

Jenny was hovering in the hallway as Tom finished his bath. She sensed that for some reason Tom was reluctant to return Peter Philips' call. She also knew that despite Tom's denial, something was troubling him, and she was sure that it stemmed from when he completed the extension on the Philips place. Maybe Tom expected something to go wrong. He was a bit of a worrier when it came to his work; he was always telling her that unless he kept a close eye on his employees they were prone to cut corners. Well, if anything had gone wrong, Jenny was sure it could be sorted out. Tom was as honest as the day was long about his business activities, his reputation meant a lot to him.

She called out to remind Tom about the phone call as he emerged from the bathroom, and was relieved when he replied that he was about to do it from the bedroom phone.

Reluctantly Tom dialled the number and waited; the sound of the phone ringing at the other end seemed to go on forever. After what seemed an age he heard somebody pick up the receiver. "Hello, Peter Philips speaking."

Tom took a deep breath. He could feel himself beginning to break out in a cold sweat; any second now Peter would challenge him to provide an explanation for what had happened. "Tom Hall here, returning your call." Forcing himself to stay calm he continued. "How can I help you, Peter?"

Downstairs Jenny heard Tom speaking. After the initial formalities he lapsed into silence, no doubt listening to the reason for Peter wanting to speak to him, and eventually she heard him say, "I think that can be arranged." Tom's voice was relaxed and Jenny immediately sensed there was no longer cause for concern. There! She had been right all along, he was chatting away upstairs, just like his old self. Whatever problem Tom had was now solved, and they could get back to normal.

"Hello Tom, thank you so much for returning my call, I am in a spot of bother and I wonder if you could help me out?" A huge sense of relief washed over Tom as he listened to Peter explain his reason for wanting to speak to him. He realised that far from being in trouble, he was being asked to do Peter a favour. Fiona had ordered new fitted wardrobes for their bedroom and they were being delivered in two days' time. Unfortunately Peter had arranged to play golf that day after promising her that he would strip out all the old fittings ready for the new ones the minute that they received a delivery date. Fiona had gone berserk when he had told her he was playing golf and could not keep his promise. It had only been when Peter suggested that they asked Tom if he could do the job that Fiona had calmed down. Tom could hear alarm bells ringing in his head; the last thing he wanted was to be alone with Fiona again. He would have to tell Peter he was sorry but at such short notice he would be unable to help. Maybe they could find somebody else to do the job. But deep down Tom knew it would be impossible for Peter to find anyone else at this late stage, but at least he would have avoided a tricky situation. It came as quite a shock when he heard himself say, "I am sure that can be arranged."

As he drove into the Philips' driveway Tom noticed that the garage door was wide open and that Peter's car had gone; he had obviously already left for his day out at golf. Tom selected the tools he thought would be required for the job in hand and made his way round to the front door. The sound of somebody hoovering told him that Fiona was doing her housework. Nervously Tom rang the front door bell and waited. Either Fiona couldn't hear him over the noise of the cleaner or she had decided to make him wait. He rang the bell again, this time for a longer period, but still no reply. It had suddenly become quite overcast and was just beginning to rain so Tom decided to walk round to the back of the house and try the rear entrance. He had barely got round there and opened the door when he heard Fiona switch off the cleaner and call out, "Is that you, Tom? Put the kettle on, there's a dear, we will have a hot drink before you start." Start what? Thought Tom as he filled the kettle.

Fiona entered the kitchen and greeted Tom with a smile, chatting away to him as if nothing had ever happened between them while she busied herself making their coffee. Tom answered her questions politely as she enquired after Jenny and his family; it was plain that Fiona wanted to forget about their previous encounter and was making small talk to hide her embarrassment. Well, if that's what she wanted, that was all right with him. He could now relax and do the job he was being paid to do, but he couldn't help feeling just a little disappointed.

The morning passed quickly enough. Tom had stripped out all the old bedroom fittings and loaded them onto his lorry. By now it was raining heavily, and for the second time of working at the Philips' residence he was getting soaked. With the room now empty, apart from the bedside cabinets and the bed itself, Tom's work was almost complete. He removed his wet shirt and hung it over the radiator under the window to dry while he collected his tools together. At least he was inside in the warm. Peter was probably in the middle of some golf course right now, getting drenched. Humming away to himself, Tom was unaware that he was being watched.

Fiona stood in the doorway admiring Tom's naked torso; years of manual labour had given him a highly toned and muscular physique. She could feel her pulse begin to quicken as she silently withdrew along the hallway into the bathroom.

The thickness of the carpet drowned out all sound as Fiona re-entered the room. Tom was standing with his back to the door looking out of the window. The sight of him still without his shirt on made her pulse start to race again; how so unlike Peter with his flabby arms and potbelly. Sensing he was not alone, Tom turned to meet her gaze. Fiona was standing in the doorway wrapped in a bath towel; in one hand she held a bottle of wine and in the other, two empty glasses. Her hair was dripping wet and as she stepped forward she left her wet footprints on the carpet. Tom stood there unable to speak; confused by all the thoughts racing through his head, he knew that he must repel her advances at all costs otherwise he was lost. Tom watched her place the wine and glasses on the bedside cabinet and allow the bath towel to slip to the floor before she moved quickly across the room and kissed him on the lips. Fiona placed her still wet hands on Tom's naked chest and slowly ran them up over his shoulders until they met round the back of his neck. The aroma from her naked body was too much for Tom to resist.

Fiona smiled. "You have been very patient and worked hard this morning. I thought you might like a little refreshment."

They made love for an hour with the wine left untouched, the wind and rain beating on the window encouraging them to renew their efforts with its every flurry, until a sudden crash at the side of the house startled them back to reality. Fiona grabbed her discarded towel off the floor and motioned Tom to stay where he was, before disappearing downstairs to investigate.

Alone in the bedroom Tom stood nervously listening. Had Peter returned unexpectedly? Panic began to set in. How would he explain the fact that Fiona was wandering about the house naked while he was in a similar state upstairs? The obvious answer would be to put some clothes on quick. Grabbing his trousers, Tom nearly over-balanced in his haste to put them on, and stumbling towards the window he ended up with his nose pressed up against the glass staring out at the street below. But apart from the wind and rain, all was quiet. There was not a car or a sign of anybody in sight.

Tom heard the back door open and close. Fiona had re-entered the house and he began to relax a little. There was movement downstairs in the kitchen and he was anxious to find out what had been going on.

Fiona was coming back up the stairs as Tom peered over the banisters; she was carrying a plate of sandwiches. "That bloody garage door will be the death of me," she laughed. "Peter must have been in such a hurry to get to his golf this morning he forgot to close the damn thing, and he's taken the remote control with him. If any of the neighbours have seen me out there in this weather with no clothes on trying to close the damn thing they will think I've flipped.

The food was a welcome distraction after all the excitement; they had not realised just how hungry they were. Tom poured out two glasses of wine and handed one to Fiona. "Drink this," he said, "I think we both need it."

"Well I do," giggled Fiona as she pushed Tom back onto the bed and straddled him.

Her swinging leg caught the half empty bottle of wine, spilling it over onto the carpet, the deep red of the claret seeping into its pile. Time enough to explain how it got there later; for now she must concentrate on more important matters. Searching for Tom with both hands Fiona gently lowered herself on to him. Moving her pelvis slowly backwards and forwards, Fiona encouraged Tom to participate, her rhythm steadily increasing as she felt Tom responding. Suddenly they were interrupted for the second time that morning.

The sound of the phone at the side of the bed echoed round the sparsely furnished room. Fiona rolled over onto her back, dragging Tom with her as she reached out and lifted the receiver. She placed her hand over the mouthpiece before turning to Tom. "If you stop now I will kill you," she hissed.

Tom tried hard to concentrate on the task in hand and at the same time listen to Fiona's part of the conversation. "Oh hello, how are you? What now? I don't think you should actually. Well, you know what Peter's like and I've got the builder in at the moment, hang on a second ..." Fiona grinned at Tom; she clenched her buttocks to get a firmer grip on him, urging him to speed up. Satisfied he was now fully focused she returned to her conversation. "You and Peter are not exactly bosom buddies; if he came home and found you here it would put him in a bad mood for the rest of the day. OK, see you tomorrow then, bye."

Fiona replaced the phone on its stand and turned her full attention to Tom. He certainly had more stamina than Peter; it had been a long time since she'd gained so much satisfaction from her love-making. Peter by now would have dropped off to sleep and be snoring his head off.

The thought of the risk she was taking and the consequences should Peter ever find out seemed to spur her on. Fiona grabbed Tom firmly round the neck and thrust her tongue deep into his mouth. The feeling was electrifying, and she could feel Tom's whole body vibrating as if he had just been plugged into the national grid. For a second the momentum of their lovemaking was thrown off balance forcing them to part. Frantically they searched for each other as they struggled to regain their rhythm, until finally they were spent.

They lay there in each other's arms, Fiona content and satisfied, Tom racked with guilt, unable to resist the compelling but exciting hold this woman had over him. After what seemed to be an age, Tom turned to Fiona and asked her who had been on the phone earlier.

"Oh that was my sister, she wanted to pop round to see me, but I put her off. You heard me tell her I had got the builder in."

Tom had a quick shower to remove the smell of Fiona from his body before venturing downstairs where he found her busy preparing the evening meal for when Peter came home; she had combed her hair and dressed herself in the little frock she had worn the last time they had been in the kitchen together. She smiled as he entered. "I think you should move your lorry from the driveway, Tom. Why don't you park it round the corner at the rear of the house and come back for a coffee before you go?"

Tom re-entered the house to find Fiona was leaning over the kitchen stove placing a tray of potatoes on the top shelf of the oven. Unaware that she was being watched she closed the door and bent over to adjust the temperature. For a moment Tom was transfixed. The sight of Fiona bending over the stove re-ignited his passion, and as she turned to place her oven gloves on the table he moved up behind her and grabbed her round the waist. Fiona pushed herself into him, and laughed as she felt him harden. Like two naughty children they rocked together from side to side, Fiona making a half-hearted attempt to escape from Tom's grasp, Tom determined to hold on. The more she squirmed the louder she giggled, until they lost their balance and fell across the kitchen table.

They lay there panting, trying to control their laughter before lapsing into silence.

Fiona could feel Tom's hands moving slowly up the back of her thighs until he found her opening; gently he caressed her until he sensed she was ready.

Fiona let out a sigh of contentment; what was it about this man that made her risk all for a morning's pleasure? It had been a long time since she had been with a man who could satisfy her needs so fully. Together in harmony they made love on the kitchen table.

The phone ringing in the lounge disturbed them for the second time that day, but they ignored it; nothing was going to be allowed to disturb their moment of passion.

"I think I am in love with you, Tom Hall," Fiona said simply, "and I'm ready now."

Tom increased his thrust; he was almost at bursting point.

The whirr of the garage door as it started to open caused him to momentarily pause. Fiona, sensing Tom's hesitation, encouraged him to continue. "Trust me, Tom, you have five minutes at least before we are disturbed, then you must leave quickly by the front door," she said calmly.

Jenny was upstairs busying her self with sorting out the kids' bits and pieces ready for the morning as Tom entered the house. She called out to ask if he had had a good day; he was certainly more relaxed since speaking to Peter Philips, so perhaps now they could get back to normal. "Why don't you come up and have a shower before the boys get home?"

Tom showered for the second time that afternoon before making his way to the bedroom; he was naked except for a small towel wrapped round his waist. Jenny was lying on the bed waiting for him; she smiled and held out her hand. "Come here and make love to me, Tom, I've been missing you."

They lay there holding hands, deep in their own thoughts. Tom felt guilty but happy that he had been able to satisfy Jenny after all these weeks. Was it really possible to love two women at the same time?

Jenny felt fulfilled; it had been a long time since they had made love together, and this time Tom had surpassed himself. She was sure that from now on everything was going to be fine.

Tom and Jenny had just finished their evening meal when the phone started to ring again for the fourth time within the hour. Jenny let out a sigh of exasperation; never a day seemed to go by lately without their evenings being interrupted, normally when they were just about to eat. Tom tried his best to explain to her that although it was inconvenient, it was what kept the work coming in, which in turn put food on the table. In fact, if business kept improving at the current rate, he would have to think about taking on more men. He only had two people working for him at the moment – Charlie who was Jenny's brother and Bert the bricklayer/come odd-job man, whose politics were considerably to the left of Carl Marx. More men meant that Tom would have to spend less time grafting. Glad of the interruption from helping the boys with their homework Tom got up to answer it.

It was Peter Philips ringing to thank Tom for the work he had carried out that day. Apparently not only had Tom got Peter out of a difficult situation, because Fiona threatened to make his life hell if he insisted on going to golf, she had been so pleased with Tom's efforts that Peter wondered if he would be prepared to install the new fitted wardrobes when they arrived.

For a moment Tom hesitated, unsure whether to agree to it or not. Sensing his reluctance, Peter pressed his case for Tom to accept. He assured Tom he was prepared to pay well, however long it took, and that if Tom rendered his account for the day's efforts it would be paid immediately.

Once again, despite his misgivings, Tom found himself agreeing to something which, deep down, he knew was unwise. As he replaced the phone on its stand he wondered what was in store for him on his next visit to the Philips.

Shrugging his shoulders, he resigned himself to whatever fate had in store for him and returned to the boys and their homework. Jenny looked up from reading her woman's magazine to enquire who had phoned. "Peter Philips will soon be one of your best customers at this rate," she joked.

"Maybe," replied Tom as he tried to prevent the guilt inside him from bubbling to the surface. But he knew he would not be able to resist the temptation of continuing to work for the Philips. He was like a moth attracted to a naked flame; one day he would get burnt. For now he would take each day as it came; after all, not many men could spend the whole afternoon making love to a beautiful woman and then send her husband the bill for his labours.

15

Search

Should you have asked David Cohen a few months ago if he believed in love at first sight, or whirlwind romances, his answer would have been a definite no. Throughout his whole life he had been brought up to believe that family background was of paramount importance in any relationship, and that the only way of getting to know a person properly was over a period of time. It was these values instilled in him by his Jewish upbringing that he had adhered to, for as long as he could remember.

Yet here he was on his way to Ireland in search of his biological mother, having just asked a woman he had only known intimately for a couple of months to be his wife. Admittedly during his visits to Sea View he had met Martha many times before, but purely on a day-to-day business basis. It was only after his adoptive parents had been so tragically taken from him that they had become close. Martha would have been with him today if it had not been for her work at Sea View. Wrapped up as she was in Tom Hall's pending birthday celebrations, she had opted to stay at the home.

For some reason best known to herself, Martha showed an almost paranoid interest in Tom Hall's health; not a week went by that she did not phone to ask if he could pop up and check him over. In the end David had had to be quite firm and insist that a monthly medical for someone even as old as Tom was quite sufficient. When David had jokingly said that if Tom were going to succumb to any of the major illnesses he would have done so by now and that at his age, when it was time for him to die, he would probably go out like a light, Martha had nearly suffered a seizure; she certainly didn't appreciate his idea of a joke.

In an odd sort of way, it was Tom Hall that had brought them together.

David had been up at the home to give Tom his monthly check-up shortly after his parents' accident, followed by their sudden demise, when Martha had asked him into her office. Offering him his usual morning coffee she had come straight to the point. "Is there something troubling you, Dr David? You have been looking very tired and worried lately."

David found himself revealing all the events of the past few months to a woman who he barely knew. Of his quest to find his natural mother, the guilt he felt towards his adoptive parents for doing so, even though they were no longer alive. All of which Martha had listened to sympathetically. She thought how vulnerable and alone he looked sitting there in front of her pouring out all his troubles, and her heart warmed to him.

For the first time in her life she felt concern for another human being apart from herself. "Have you thought of enlisting the help of the Salvation Army," she enquired. "I understand they are very experienced in these matters, more so than most other tracing agencies, especially solicitors. From my dealings with them here at the home the majority of solicitors are only interested in boosting their fees. For months, every time I have phoned the home's solicitor with a query about one of the residents, I have been asked to confirm my instructions in writing, only to find out that not only have I been charged for the initial phone call, but for them receiving the follow-up letter as well."

This advice from Martha had proved to be invaluable. Within a few weeks of David contacting the Salvation Army they had given him the name of an intermediary in the Market town of Bantry in South West Ireland, hence his reason for being up in an aeroplane halfway across the Irish Sea.

David summoned the stewardess and enquired if he could have another coffee. He thought it best to keep off the alcohol, as his intention was to hire a car on arriving at the airport and he didn't want any trouble with the local police should he be stopped en route.

What would he have done without Martha? She had been a constant source of help and support. If it had not been for her he didn't know how he would have coped. Right from that very first day in her office when he had nervously asked her to have dinner with him one evening, and she – much to his surprise and delight – so readily agreed, their relationship had gone from strength to strength.

He recalled the first time she had invited him into her bed, a place he was sure very few, if any, had been in the past.

After an extraordinary good meal, plus a couple of bottles of vintage wine, Martha had advised David against driving home and suggested he stay the night.

Rebecca had always maintained that David needed the influence of a woman with a strong character. A woman that would guide him in the right direction. Martha fitted the bill perfectly. Apart from the fact that she was not Jewish, she had all the qualities that Rebecca would have yearned for to keep her son focussed on the important things in life. It had not gone down very well with her when David had decided to give up his consultancy and move into general practice. If Rebecca was alive today, David felt sure Martha would have met with her approval.

They had lain there side-by-side in Martha's bed, each trying not to let the other know how nervous they were. David, because apart from being slightly tipsy, could not recall the last time he had been in a similar situation, and Martha because she did not want to appear too eager. The outcome of tonight's little tryst could make or break her future plans.

It had been David who broke the silence. "You know, Martha, it's a long time since I have done anything like this and I hope I don't let you down."

Seeing this as a sign of David's insecurity Martha decided that unless she made a move, all would be lost. Gently she reassured him that there was nothing to be concerned about and took control of the situation. Automatically assuming the dominant roll, she led and instructed him in every aspect of their lovemaking until, exhausted but happy, they had fallen asleep in each other's arms.

The next morning while lying in bed discussing whether or not to keep their now more intimate relationship a secret, David had heard himself asking Martha to be his wife. Barely able to control her excitement she had cried "Yes, yes, yes" and promptly demanded he made love to her again. Despite his exertion from the night before, David was happy to comply.

The sound of the seat belt sign coming on and the pilot's voice over the address system jolted David back to the present; he pushed all thought of his pending nuptials to one side and concentrated on his descent onto Irish soil. As the plane circled and made its approach into County Cork airport, David wondered what surprises the next couple of days had in store for him.

The drive from the airport along the N71 towards Bantry in some strange way reminded him of his earlier trip from Eastbourne to London. Then, as now, he had been filled with anxiety. He hoped, however, that at the end of this journey the outcome would be a much happier affair. It was certainly a more beautiful and calming experience. As he drove through the rolling countryside within the shadows of the hauntingly beautiful Sheehy Mountains, David couldn't help but marvel at the beauty of Ireland. How anyone could leave this heaven on earth and choose to live in a place like London was beyond him. Approaching his destination after about an hour of driving, through what must surely be one of the most picturesque journeys he had ever undertaken, David pulled the car over to the side of the road to gather his thoughts and look down on Bantry Town. In front of him he could see the imposing building that was St Finbarrs.

Behind him on the opposite side of the road was a strangely enchanting Catholic church. With its little graveyard and dilapidated parish hall, decorated with bunting and posters advertising the forthcoming Christmas Fair, David imagined how beautiful it must look in the spring. If only Martha was with him now; he was sure she would agree that it would make an ideal setting for their impending wedding.

David decided to get out of the vehicle and walk over to the church entrance. He studied the notice board closely and made a note of the parish priest and the accompanying telephone number for future use. In his pocket was the name of the contact given to him by the Salvation Army back in England, together with the details of where he was to lodge during his stay. Everything, it would appear, had been arranged with the precision of a military exercise. If anything went wrong now, it would certainly not be the fault of the 'Sally Ann'.

David strolled back to the car, pausing only for one last look before continuing his journey to the town below. With its bustling market square filled with tiny figures going about their daily business he wondered if there was anybody else down there apart from his mother who knew the secrets of his parentage. It was too much to hope that somebody apart from her would know who his father was, or more to the point, if he were still alive. As he restarted the engine and engaged the gear to set the car in motion, he hoped the person who was to act as intermediary in bringing about the reunion with his birth mother was of sufficient sensitivity and maturity to ensure everything went smoothly.

The little tavern where it had been arranged for David to stay was pleasant enough. With its white painted stucco exterior and bow fronted windows it reminded him of how he imagined the Admiral Benbow would have looked from the book *Treasure Island*. The difference being he hoped to meet an entirely different character than that of Blind Pew.

Entering the building from the car park at the rear he was greeted by the landlord and shaken warmly by the hand. It was obvious that visitors were few and far between if the owner had time to meet all his guests personally. "Welcome to my humble establishment. Dr David Cohen, I presume."

David smiled to himself. He felt like another David from history, all those years ago in darkest Africa.

The room David had been allotted was comfortable enough, deceptively spacious considering the size of the building and nicely decorated. After a quick shower and a change of clothes, he was ready for a meal before meeting his contact.

The landlord looked up as he entered the bar. "Settled in, Sir," he enquired. " If you would like to take a seat, I will ask cook to bring you something to eat. In the meantime while you are waiting, can I get you a drink?"

The meal was plain and wholesome, just as David had expected it would be. Anyone who employed a cook instead of some fancy chef was not going to serve haute cuisine. Old-fashioned steak and kidney pie with home grown vegetables was the order of the day, washed down with a pint of thick black Irish Guinness, in contrast to the watery liquid that passed for Guinness in England.

Hunger satisfied, David sat back and surveyed his surroundings. The large room that made up for most of the ground floor space had been sub-divided into sections; the dining area where David sat, a lounge area, and a bar at the far end for those who liked to stand and enjoy their pint. David grabbed the remains of his drink and made his way past the other guests towards a rather inviting leather armchair at the far end of the lounge. Settled in, he sat back and waited for his contact to appear.

At the far end of the room, mingling with the locals, he noticed the familiar figure of the lady from the Salvation Army. With copies of The War Cry lodged firmly on her arm and her collecting tin attached to her wrist she moved from customer to customer. Standing discreetly to one side, she waited patiently for them to finish their conversation, before plying them with her wares. David realised this was probably how the Army gathered a good deal of its information. Loose tongues after a few pints would provide them with a mine of information.

He didn't have long to wait. Just as David was dozing off after his heavy meal and even heavier Guinness he felt a tap on the shoulder. He opened his eyes to see a fresh-faced youth of around 18 to 20 years of age smiling down on him. "Dr David Cohen?" The youth offered his hand to David in greeting. "I am Father Joseph O'Malley, local parish priest. Welcome to Bantry. I believe you are expecting me?"

What if this woman he had come all this way to meet suddenly changed her mind and refused to see him? What if they had nothing in common and he took an immediate dislike to her, or worse still if he did like her, and she didn't like him? David regretted now that he had resisted the temptation to indulge in a large whisky before setting out. It was only the fact that he didn't want his natural mother to think she had given birth to a chronic alcoholic that had given him the willpower to do so.

Despite the fact he was a grown man approaching middle age, with a degree in medicine, and of considerable social standing in the community, David was as nervous as a child on its first day at school. If only he had brought Martha along to hold his hand. Plucking up courage he rang the front door bell and waited.

Inside the house Sarah jumped up from her chair as if being shot from a cannon. "It's him," she said to her companion. "Why did I agree to meet him after all this time? Why didn't I let sleeping dogs lie? He is a doctor, a man of letters; I am only a poor farm girl, and we have nothing in common."

Sarah's companion looked at her. His clear blue eyes, still bright and alert despite his age, filled with love. "If he is any man at all he will respect you whatever you are, and you have lots in common; you are his mother, the same flesh and blood. Now, shall I answer the door before he changes his mind and goes back to England?"

Sarah nodded and squeezed his hand. "Thank you, yes please."

The two men stood there in the open doorway looking at one another. The older one upright and proud, his eyes unflinching, yet somehow filled with sadness and longing brought about by a lifetime of suffering. The younger man managing to stand his ground and not run away, nervous and unsure

David extended his hand to greet his host. He couldn't help thinking they had met before; there was something about him that was vaguely familiar. The handshake was warm and firm as David was ushered into the spacious hallway. "You must be David, please come in. Did you have a pleasant journey?" Realising he was beginning to ramble on, the older man motioned David to follow him into a room at the front of the house. He leaned forward to open the door and turned and looked David in the eye. "This is as difficult for your mother as it is for you. Please be patient and gentle with her, she is not a young woman anymore." With that he opened the door and ushered David into the room. "Your mother will be with you shortly; please make yourself at home."

As the door closed behind him, David surveyed the room. Large and comfortably furnished, it was adorned with photographs everywhere. He moved forward to take a closer look and gasped in amazement.

On the small coffee table was a photograph of Samuel and Rebecca standing next to a young girl of about 18 years of age. She was holding a baby in her arms. He picked it up and looked at it closely, his mind in a whirl. Clutching the picture closely to him, he moved slowly around the room studying the numerous photographs of a baby boy in various stages of its development, pictures he recognised from Samuel and Rebecca's north London home. David walked over to the mantelpiece, almost fainting, as there in front of him was a selection of photographs that were only too familiar. There was one of him on his first day at school, looking so proud in his new uniform. Another of his bar mitzvah; even one of him in his cap and gown when he had graduated from university. Completely perplexed David slumped down on the couch, the photograph of the little family group still grasped to his chest.

With his breath coming in short gasps, David felt the emotion begin to build up inside him, tears rolled down his cheeks and his shoulders shook as he sobbed silently, unable to control his feelings any longer.

David never heard the door open; the first he realised that he was not alone was when he felt a gentle hand on his shoulder. He looked up into the eyes of the woman standing in front of him and knew instantly that it was his mother. Throwing his arms round her waist, he buried his head in her bosom. Despite the advancing years she looked every bit as beautiful as her photograph. They embraced each other in silence; no words were necessary as the pain of the past ebbed from them.

How could this woman be so calm and strong when he felt so weak and vulnerable? As his mother kissed him gently on the forehead David was sure he detected the faint aroma of a large whisky.

The man framed in the doorway stood there silently looking at them clinging together. A single tear rolled down his cheek before he turned and left, closing the door quietly behind him.

16

Fear

Christmas was fast approaching and rehearsals for the annual carol service were well underway, which was more than could be said for Malcolm's relationship with Pearl. It was some months since their first meeting and things were at a standstill. When he had offered her a lift home after choir practice that first evening he had been a little surprised at her reaction when he had leant across to give her a kiss on her cheek; she had visibly stiffened and drawn away from him.

At the time he had put it down to the fact that they had only just met. Since then, however, although it was obvious she liked his company, whenever he tried to make physical contact with her she had shied away. He knew her reaction disturbed her as much as it did him, because of the way she kept apologising. The last time it had happened Pearl had burst into tears and suggested that perhaps it would be better all round if they ended their friendship. Stunned by her comment, Malcolm asked if that was what she really wanted.

Pearl stood there like a lost soul shaking her head and trying not to cry. It was at that moment Malcolm realised the last thing he wanted was for them to part company; he could not bear the thought of not ever seeing her again.

Gathering her in his arms he held her to him and explained that there was not a problem in this world they could not solve together if they really wanted to. It was while Malcolm was holding her that Pearl revealed the secret she had kept all to herself since her youth. The secret that she had been afraid to tell anyone, not even her mother.

Malcolm listened quietly as Pearl recounted to him the event that had happened to her when she was 14 years of age.

Pearl had just left the school building on her way home from the annual disco, at around 11.15, and was in high spirits; not only had she had the best night of her life so far, she had danced with Adrian Parker, not once, but three times. All the girls in her class, if not the whole school, had the hots for Adrian. Tall and muscular with long blonde hair, he was not only the captain of the school football team, but the athletic and cricket teams as well. Two years older than Pearl and in his last term before he left to make his own way in life, she hadn't thought for one moment that he would dance with her, let alone three times. She could still smell the aroma of almonds that seemed to be impregnated in his clothes and feel the closeness of his body as she walked across the school yard towards the gate.

Her mother had insisted that she would only allow Pearl to go to the school disco on the strict understanding that she was brought home by one of the other girls' parents or that she came home in a taxi. But it was a warm night; what was the harm in walking the short distance from the school gate to her house? The streets were well lit and there were lots of other girls and boys making their own way home and she wanted to fantasise about Adrian Parker. He had held her so close to him as they danced that she could feel how aroused he was. When he had moved his hand up from her waist to touch her breast she had nearly wet herself with excitement.

For a moment, as Pearl made her way across the school yard, she was lost in a little dream world of her own. A world where Adrian Parker was her knight in shining armour, astride a huge white charger, on his way to rescue her from the 'evil baron'.

"Pearly, Pearly, over here." For a few seconds Pearl thought she was still daydreaming, but no somebody was definitely calling her name. "Pearly, Pearly, I'm over here." Pearl peered across the yard; it was now in complete darkness. The caretaker had obviously thought that everyone had left the premises and turned off all the exterior lights. Only the light radiating through the windows of the main hall allowed her to see anything at all. Inside somebody was rearranging the tables and chairs ready for the morning assembly. Through the gloom Pearl could just make out a shadowy figure over by the cycle sheds. Her heart skipped a beat as she recognised the tall handsome profile of Adrian Parker. What a story she would have to tell if she was escorted home by the school's sports captain no less? Pearl ran over to greet him; she was somewhat surprised to see two other figures lurking in the shadows, but was sure she recognised them as Adrian's companions from earlier in the evening. If they were friends of Adrian they would be OK, he would look after her.

Pearl could feel Adrian's hands start to explore her body. He kissed her passionately as he grasped her to him. Pearl was in heaven. The story was getting better; all the other girls would be green with envy that she had been snogging Adrian Parker.

Suddenly Pearl began to feel uncomfortable. Adrian was getting a little too rough with his wandering hands, and he was beginning to hurt her. She tried to pull away from him but his grip tightened. He was really hurting her now and he had a strange look in his eyes. "Stop it, Adrian, you're hurting me. Stop please."

"You're gagging for it, Pearly, you know you are." His voice was husky and strange and Pearl began to panic. She struggled to get away from him but he was too strong for her. Somewhere behind her she could hear footsteps approaching. Pearl breathed a sigh of relief; the caretaker must have heard her cries for help and was coming to her assistance. There seemed to be two pairs of hands grabbing at her, but instead of helping her to safety they were forcing her to the floor. Her relief turned to terror at the realisation that her so-called saviour was in fact Adrian's companions. Something was being forced into her mouth in an attempt to stifle her cries for help. It smelt of almonds. As Pearl lapsed into unconsciousness, all she could feel was the pain as first Adrian and then the others raped her.

Malcolm stood there stunned. Everything now made sense, why Pearl had been so afraid of physical contact, why she hated being alone with him in the dark. He must have been a fool not to have realised there was more to her fears than just girlish embarrassment.

Since revealing the terrible secret that she had kept to herself for so long, Pearl had felt a lot better. Malcolm had been so sympathetic and understanding that she agreed to start afresh with their relationship.

Little by little the pair of them rekindled their feelings for each other to the extent that Pearl had agreed to spend her next weekend off with Malcolm in his apartment. Although she was apprehensive, deep down she was looking forward to it. As the weekend approached, however, Pearl began to have second thoughts, but she had promised Malcolm and was determined not to disappoint him.

Entering Malcolm's flat that Friday evening was the bravest thing Pearl had ever done and she was desperate that her anxiety should not spoil the weekend. Malcolm for his part appeared to be totally relaxed. Taking her things up to his bedroom, he was at pains to explain that for their first night he would be sleeping downstairs in the lounge. Despite her assurances that this would not be necessary, he had insisted.

The evening itself turned out to be very pleasant. Malcolm cooked a lovely meal after which they sat and shared a bottle of wine together before settling down on the sofa to watch television until it was time to retire for the night.

Pearl had not felt so relaxed for ages as she showered and prepared herself for bed, half wishing that Malcolm would join her and half fearing that he might. She quickly changed into the little nightie that she had bought especially for the occasion and jumped into Malcolm's double divan. She barely had time to snuggle down and reflect on the events of the day when there was a tap on the door and Malcolm entered. Pearl could feel herself begin to shake with fear, but she knew there was no need; Malcolm would never force her into something she was not ready for. Pearl was certain of that.

She heard him approaching as she lay there hugging the duvet, pretending to be asleep. Malcolm walked across the room to where she lay trembling and bent over to kiss her gently on the forehead before leaving the room, closing the door quietly behind him.

As she made her way downstairs, Pearl could hear that Malcolm was up and moving around. The smell of frying bacon and fresh ground coffee greeted her as she entered the lounge. "I hope you're hungry, Pearl, otherwise I've wasted my time getting up early." Pearl smiled and nodded. She still felt a little sheepish from the night before, when she had feigned sleep, but Malcolm showed no sign of having been put out so she decided to put on a brave face. That Saturday morning, Pearl sat down with Malcolm in his tiny kitchen and enjoyed her first ever breakfast with a man who was not an actual member of her family.

Saturday turned out to be a lovely day for the time of the year. Pearl and Malcolm walked along the seafront hand in hand. Eastbourne was such a beautiful place to be when you had someone to share it with. They stopped for coffee on the pier before having lunch in one of the many little restaurants in the centre of town, followed by a visit to the local theatre to take in a matinee performance of the Christmas pantomime. Pearl was glowing with happiness, and when Malcolm told her he had booked a table in the Grand Hotel for their evening meal it completed a perfect day.

Later that evening when they had returned to the flat, Malcolm poured out two brandies; a large one for himself and a smaller one for Pearl. Despite Pearl's reaction the night before when he had entered her room to say goodnight, he thought the weekend so far had been a stunning success. Pearl seemed more relaxed now than at any time since they had first met and he was determined not to spoil it. He handed the smaller brandy to Pearl and sat down on the sofa, patting the cushion at his side for Pearl to join him. They sat there in silence sipping their drinks, each wrapped up in their own thoughts about the success of the day.

After what seemed an eternity Pearl placed the glass containing the remains of her brandy on the little coffee table by her side and turned to face Malcolm. "Instead of sleeping down here on your own, why don't you join me in the double bed?"

Malcolm looked at her intently. "Are you sure? I do not want you to feel pressurised into something you are not ready for."

Pearl nodded. "I'm sure." Taking hold of his hand, she led him up the stairs.

Together they undressed and showered. Pearl had never shared a shower with anyone other than her mother, let alone a man, and the sight of Malcolm naked aroused feelings that she had never experienced before. For all the reaction she received from Malcolm, however, they might just as well have been brother and sister,

Laughing and giggling like two teenagers they lay together side-by-side in the large double bed, cuddling and caressing each other until Malcolm reached over and turned out the light. He could sense Pearl begin to shake and as he reached out to touch her face he could feel that she was sweating. He kissed her on the lips, whispered "good night sweetheart" and turned over and went to sleep.

Pearl lay there in the darkness. She could hear Malcolm's shallow breathing. How could he be so laid back and calm about everything? She was so lucky to have met him. It must have been fate that threw them together. Well, she was damned if she was going to lose him just because of Adrian Parker. As she fell asleep she dreamt of being in Grandma's kitchen turning the handle of the mangle for her as she did the weekly wash, only instead of Grandpa's shirts passing through the rollers each time she turned the handle it was Adrian Parkers genitals.

The church service was packed, but then it usually was on a Sunday morning. The population of Eastbourne was mainly made up of the older generation who were now nearing the end of their time on this earth; they were anxious to show that they had led a blameless life, in case there was any truth in the afterlife theory. Also the choir had been on great form. Malcolm in particular was in fine voice. Pearl always felt a special thrill every time she heard him sing. His voice was the first thing that had attracted her to him when he joined the choir.

After church they took a stroll along the seafront before deciding to splash out and lunch at the Grand Hotel for the second time that weekend. It was during the meal that Malcolm asked Pearl if she would like to return to Sea View that evening or spend another night with him at the flat. Pearl pondered for a moment; she was on duty early Monday morning and should really return to her own room in the home, but deep down she wanted to stay with Malcolm for as long as possible. Seeing her dilemma Malcolm suggested that if she agreed, they could spend the evening at his place and if she decided to stay he would drop her off at Sea View early Monday morning.

Pearl lay there curled up in a ball with her knees tucked up under her chin. The bed was so warm and comfortable, but above all she felt so safe in it. She could hear Malcolm in the shower singing quietly to himself in that lovely deep baritone voice of his. Any minute now he would be joining her for the last time that weekend, it was back to work tomorrow. She didn't know how long it would be before she was due another weekend off. But at least they had tonight, and they could cuddle up together, just like last night.

Pearl wished with all her heart that she had been able to let Malcolm make love to her. Each time they had tried she had started to shake with fear and her body had gone rigid. It must have been so frustrating for Malcolm, yet he had never reproached her in any way, or made her feel guilty for calling a halt to his advances. Quite the reverse, he had apologised for being too hasty and eager, telling her that he was happy just to lay there close to her. Pearl could feel the tears well up inside her as she recalled his concern. She knew that one day they would make love like other couples. Malcolm had reassured her of that fact and she believed him.

Pearl was suddenly aware that the water from the shower had stopped running and that Malcolm was no longer singing.

The sound of the bedroom door opening was preceded by the smell of Malcolm's body lotion. There was no mistaking Chanel's 'Pour Monsieur'. It was such a lovely feeling lying there, knowing he was about to join her. As Pearl turned her head slightly so that she could watch him enter the room, he blew her a kiss and told her to stay where she was. "You look so comfortable, don't move."

Malcolm hopped into bed beside her; he reached over to retrieve his book from the cabinet on her side of the bed and started to read. Pearl felt so contented and secure, she was sure not another man in this world would be as patient understanding as Malcolm.

It must have been nearly an hour before Malcolm put his book down. Pearl lay there in the foetal position with her back towards him, quite happy to watch the shadows dancing on the bedroom wall as he lay beside her, feeling the warmth of his body while he read his book. They reminded her of happier times when she was a little girl, lying in bed with her grandparents, listening to them read her a story from her favourite book, days when she had not a care in the world. The shadows on the wall were no longer moving and Pearl could feel herself drifting off to sleep. The brandy was doing its work.

Pearl was aware that Malcolm had turned towards her to replace his book, his left arm circling her waist as he snuggled into her. With his free hand he gently massaged inside the back of her thighs. She sighed with content as she felt him gently exploring her. Wondering why he had not turned off the bedroom light, she tried to turn to face him but he gently pushed her back to face the wall.

"Stay as you are," he whispered. "Are you OK?" Pearl nodded, feeling safe and secure in his embrace. Malcolm continued to caress her from behind, his large gentle hands seeking out and finding her points of passion. The more he fondled her the more relaxed she became. Her knees were still pulled up tightly under her chin and Pearl began to tingle every time Malcolm touched her.

And then he was inside her. His rhythm slow and firm with short gentle thrusts that increased as she relaxed. The tears rolled down Pearls cheeks. Malcolm paused, concerned that he was hurting her. But Pearl was crying with happiness, begging him to continue; she knew that she had conquered all her fears. Adrian Parker would never haunt her again. As she lay there at the end of the most wonderful weekend of her life, Pearl couldn't help thinking of her mother. Not only had she met a man she would be proud to take home and introduce to Joyce, but she had obeyed her instructions and kept her knees together the whole time.

17

The Letter

A retirement home for the elderly is not the ideal place to make long-term friendships and since Robert passed away Tom had felt very lonely. It was five years since that fateful day. Not long after he had thrown a wobbly in the lounge and told the whole world and his wife that he was gay.

Tom had admired him for that. Despite it being well into the 21st century there were still plenty of people around who frowned on same sex partnerships. Brigadier Jack Holland for a start. But he was no longer with us either, thank God. What a bloody hypocrite he'd turned out to be. Forever boasting about his military service and his prowess with the ladies, only to find out in the end it was all a tissue of lies. Brigadier Holland indeed, what a turn up for the book that was when he died. All those years of telling everyone what a hero he was in the Falklands only to find out from his relatives at his wake that he had never been in any of the armed forces. But the biggest surprise of all was the reason why.

Uncle Jack, according to the pleasant young naval officer at the wake, and who turned out to be Jack Holland's nephew, had always wanted to serve in the armed forces. Back in the unenlightened days of his youth, however, certain categories of people were discouraged from enlisting, especially in the Royal Navy, the so-called senior service, the main reason being if you happened to be homosexual. Nowadays, of course, they took anybody, as long as you were warm and still breathing you were welcomed with open arms. All this, however, didn't stop Uncle Jack and his preferences from being a close-kept family secret. Jack's nephew shrugged his shoulders; he couldn't understand what all the fuss had been about, as he said, "There are lots of us around these days; the sad thing is Uncle Jack hid behind a façade of make believe and fabrication in order to cover up his deep sense of rejection, instead of facing up to things."

Well, Robert had faced up to things, and as far as Tom was concerned Robert proved to be more of a man in the end than Jack Holland had ever been, whatever their preferences in life.

Tom was glad that he had made his peace with Robert. It would have been awful if Robert had left this world before they had had a chance to make up. They had been friends ever since the first day when Tom arrived at Sea View 15 years before, and 15 years was a long time to know someone, especially when you were not introduced until you were turned 80.

The walk down to the seafront had cleared the air. Tom had apologised for forever going on about Jenny, which triggered the outburst in the first place, and Robert had apologised for being so sensitive about the whole affair.

They had sat together on the promenade while Robert related to Tom how he had first met Simon, right through up until the day he died, and Tom had listened, not once interrupting or mentioning Jenny. That final heart-to-heart was the last time he and Robert had walked to the seafront together, and Tom missed those walks. Over the past few years his legs had become steadily weaker and weaker. Now he could just about manage to move around his room with the aid of his walking frame. It was a bugger getting older, all the bits and pieces started to cease functioning. Although he had been extremely lucky in that respect, some, if not most of the others in the home were in a far worse state than him. At least he could still dress himself and attend to his own personal needs. Thankfully Robert had been quite agile right to the end. When he recalled that day he was quite envious of the way that Robert died.

Tom had arranged to meet Robert in the lounge at ten o'clock that morning after breakfast. Normally they would have breakfasted together in the dining room, a habit that had developed from the first day of Tom's arrival at Sea View, but occasionally Robert wanted to be alone and Tom respected that. But it was now twenty past ten and there was no sign of him, which was unusual, because Robert was a stickler for punctuality, a quality shared by the both of them, unlike the modern generation. Spying Pearl out in the hallway, Tom called out to her, "I don't suppose you have seen Robert on your travels, have you Pearl?"

Pearl hesitated; she was on her way to see Martha about the weekly duty rota, and if she kept her waiting without a good excuse there would be hell to pay. But sod her, let her wait; it was not often Tom wanted anything, and his needs were greater than Martha Branigan. She would just look in to see what all the fuss was about.

Pearl could see Tom was getting agitated. Normally at this time of the morning he and Robert were engaged in a game of chess. Popping her head round the door Pearl asked him what the problem was. "I arranged to meet Robert at ten, but he hasn't arrived yet. I wondered if you had seen him?"

Pearl shook her head. "No I haven't, Tom, would you like me to go up to his room to see if he is alright. Better still, why don't you come with me? We can take the lift to save your legs. Knowing Robert I expect he has either forgotten he has arranged to meet you, or has dropped off to sleep."

Pearl tapped gently on the door before entering. The room was in semi darkness, with the curtains still closed from the night before. In the half-light she could see that Robert's bed had not been slept in. Tom by now had managed to catch up and was standing in the doorway. He was about to remark that nobody was at home when he saw the outline of Robert slumped in the chair by the window. The silly old fool must have fallen asleep.

Pearl moved across the room and drew the curtains; she didn't like the look of this. As she placed her hand on Roberts's forehead Pearl could feel that he was quite cold. Reaching out she grabbed his wrist and felt for a pulse; there was none.

Turning to Tom, she said, "Don't come any closer, Tom, this looks serious. Take your time and go and fetch Martha Branigan.

The minute that Tom had left the room Pearl quickly took stock of the situation. It was plain to see that Robert had been there all night; he was still dressed in the clothes she had seen him in the day before and apart from the unused bed there was an untouched cup of coffee on the bedside cabinet. She noticed a cigarette holder on the table beside his chair and thought how strange; to her knowledge Robert had never smoked.

The sound of footsteps scurrying along the corridor told her that Martha Branigan was on her way. Well, Martha could take over now, that was what she got paid for. Just as she was about to move away and allow Martha to take command, Pearl spotted something clasped in Roberts's hand; it was a folded sheet of paper. Strange how she hadn't noticed it before while searching for his pulse earlier. As she removed it from his grasp Pearl glanced at it briefly, realising it was a letter wrapped round a photograph of a young man. With no time to read it before Martha's arrival, Pearl thrust it into her uniform pocket and turned to meet her superior.

Martha Branigan stood in the doorway red faced and panting for breath, closely followed by an equally breathless Tom. "What's up? Tom said you wanted me up here straight away."

"It's Robert Downing. I'm sure he's dead; it looks as if he's been here all night."

Martha paled. "Christ that means nobody checked up on him last night. Who was on duty?"

"You were," replied Pearl, "it was my night off."

Martha hesitated; she had been exceptionally busy yesterday, what with half the staff away with the flu and the others only doing half of what they were supposed to. Was it any wonder she had overlooked checking on Robert. "Never mind who's to blame now," she said briskly, "go and phone Dr David Cohen; tell him it's an emergency, while I sort things out here."

As soon as Pearl had left the room Martha began to take stock of the situation. If she weren't careful there would have to be an enquiry into the circumstances of Roberts's death. How, for instance, was he allowed to remain undetected for so long and why he was still dressed in his day clothes. Even worse, when he was eventually discovered, why was it not until after ten o'clock the following morning? All of these things Martha thought she would be able to explain with a little co-operation from Pearl and Doctor David, but she needed time to think. For now she must tidy up things here, get rid of the cold cup of coffee for a start, and what was that disgusting thing on the table? Turning round, Martha realised Tom was standing by the table watching all that was going on. "That will be all, Thomas, you'd better go back into the lounge while I look after things here. On your way pop into the office and ask Pearl to give you a brandy from my cupboard, I'm sure you have had a nasty shock. And while you are at it tell her to dispose of this disgusting thing."

Tom left the room in a daze. Fancy Robert dying like that. He hoped when it was his turn to die it would be as peaceful. It was at times like these that he wondered how much longer it would be before he did go. After all, what was the point of living any longer? He had lost his only friend, and most of his family were either dead or living abroad. Jenny had promised him that one day they would be together again. What was it she had said? He struggled to remember; even his memory was going now. Something about telling him when it was time to go.

Tom arrived at Martha's office just as Pearl had finished her call to Dr Cohen. He greeted her with a faint smile. "Martha said you were to give me a large brandy, but if it's all the same to you I would prefer a scotch."

"Are you alright, Tom?" Pearl sounded anxious. It was a bloody great shock for her and she was less than half his age.

Tom smiled ruefully. "I'm OK. When you get to my time of life you accept these sort of things. It doesn't make it any easier, but you accept them."

"Here, get this down you." Pearl handed Tom a more than generous whisky. Her hands were shaking causing her to spill some of the contents onto Martha's desk. Reaching into her pocket for a handkerchief to wipe up the mess, the letter and photograph she had removed from Roberts's hand fluttered to the floor.

Tom waited patiently while Pearl scanned through the contents. Without raising her eyes she held out the accompanying photograph towards him. As he studied the handsome face smiling back at him, Tom knew instantly that it was Robert's partner Simon. Before he could comment, Pearl finished reading the letter and handed it over to Tom.

'My Dearest Robert,

By the time you read this I will no longer be with you. The one great sadness in life is that, as in any partnership, one of you has to die before the other. I could not leave this world, however, without thanking you for the love you have given me over the past 40 years. Please, please, do not be sad at my passing. Without you, life for me would have been nothing. With you, I have lived a full life, crammed with love and laughter. The care and devotion you have shown to me during my illness proved that I was right in my choice of partner.

You see, Robert, when we first met in that dance hall all those years ago, it was not entirely by accident. I had seen you there on previous occasions and had set my heart on you. My nervousness, masked by my endless jokes and flamboyant dress, enabled me to take the plunge and approach you, a decision for which I have thanked God every day. Be happy my darling Robert. When the pain of my passing subsides continue life again, until we meet in another world.

My dearest wish is that you eventually find a true and loyal friend to ease the pain as you continue your journey through life

*Goodbye,
Yours forever*

Simon.'

By the time he finished reading Pearl could see that Tom was trembling. Gently she took the letter from him and walked over to the electric fire on the office wall. Together with the photograph she held them over the hot element until they burst into flames, before tossing the hot ashes into the metal wastepaper bin under Martha's desk. "I hope they are together now, don't you Tom?" Pearl wiped a tear from her eyes. "Have another whisky. As a matter of fact I think I will join you. Sod Martha Branigan! If she doesn't like it she can go to hell.

After two whiskies, Tom was feeling a bit wobbly. He thought it best if he made his way back to his room for a lie down. It was not yet lunchtime and he was pissed already, but at least it was at Martha's expense and not his own and Robert would have appreciated the irony of the situation.

Tom removed his jacket and hung it on the chair by the side of his bed. Something in the pocket caught his attention; it was a cigarette holder. Wondering how the hell it had got there he placed it in the drawer of the bedside cabinet, lay back and dropped off to sleep, to dream of Jenny and all the people he had known throughout his long life. So many of them now only in his dreams, so few in life.

18

Boots

It certainly was a beautiful day for late December. Even so, the wind was bitter, belying the winter sunshine, and Malcolm had advised her to wrap up warm for the journey. Pearl decided to wear her new two-piece suit and simulated fur wrap, together with her black leather boots. The skirt of the two-piece was a touch on the short side and the knee- length boots rather too heavy for her liking but at least they would keep her warm. Especially if she was to spend the morning walking around town. And anyway Malcolm said the boots made her look sexy.

The journey up to London had been quite pleasant. Not nearly as crowded as Pearl would have expected considering it was Boxing Day. She and Malcolm had managed to find a compartment on the train all to themselves, which allowed them to indulge in the silly games Pearl used to play when her grandfather was alive. Malcolm for his part was quite happy to go along with her. It had been a long, long time since he had played eye spy, or counted how many houses had green curtains. But anything that so obviously gave Pearl a thrill was OK with him. In fact when the train eventually pulled into London Malcolm was quite disappointed; it was his turn to choose the next game. He had been granted an interview with the choirmaster of Westminster Abbey and was anxious to make a good impression. The silly games played on the journey up from Eastbourne seemed to have helped him to relax and take his mind off what was in effect an audition to join the choir.

Pearl had not enjoyed such a morning for as long as she could remember and was glad that she had agreed to go along for moral support, even if she was destined to walk the streets of London on her own for a couple of hours. Malcolm had been at pains to explain to Pearl that, although he was glad of her company, he would rather she wasn't around when the actual audition took place as he felt her presence would make him nervous. Why he should think that was beyond Pearl; in her opinion Malcolm had a beautiful voice. Westminster would be the lucky ones if he did join them. But if that's how he felt so be it. It would be a good excuse for her to spend a couple of hours wandering round the sales to see if she could pick up a bargain, maybe replace her boots with a lighter pair.

Pearl would have liked to remain in London well into the evening, so that she and Malcolm could take in the illuminations, perhaps even have dinner in one of the many swanky restaurants in town, but with Tom Hall's birthday looming, she was wanted back at Sea View. Martha Branigan would kick up a fuss if she were not back on duty in time to help with the last-minute preparations. Doubtless there would be plenty more opportunities to see the lights now that the health and safety brigade had been well and truly thwarted. Pearl smiled to herself as she recalled Tom saying he thought he would never live to see the day when common sense returned to this country.

Living on the south coast certainly had its benefits compared to London. Everything in Eastbourne seemed so fresh and open by comparison. Walking along Oxford Street everyone seemed in such a hurry, even though they were only going shopping. The one thing Eastbourne did appear to have in common with London were the drug addicts and drunks. Sitting on the pavements in front of the shops, begging for money, there seemed to be no way of escaping them. How sad that with only just over a year to go before we entered the fourth decade of the 21st century, people were still living rough and having to beg for a living.

Pearl's thoughts momentarily strayed back to Malcolm; she wondered if his audition was going well, or whether his nerves would eventually get the better of him. Her brief lack of concentration almost caused Pearl to fall as she tripped over the outstretched leg of the drunk propped up against the shop window, scattering the contents of his can of strong lager all over the pavement. His curses drew sidelong glances from passers-by, but nobody intervened to enquire if she needed assistance; lowering their heads they scurried on about their business. Pearl stammered her apologies, the smell of stale urine causing her to recoil in disgust.

The wretched figure in front of her raised his head to see who had deprived him of his last drink. His lips were covered in sores from years of drug abuse and his long tangled hair, which Pearl guessed was once blond, hung over his face. As he opened his mouth to continue his tirade against his perceived attacker, Pearl caught a glimpse of broken and rotting teeth. A pair of clear blue eyes that were vaguely familiar stared mockingly back at her. Something inside made Pearl feel uneasy and frightened. Hastily opening her purse she grabbed a handful of loose change and tossed it in the direction of the huddled figure in an effort to placate his aggressive manner, and at the same time wishing that she had remained back at Westminster with Malcolm.

The piecing blue eyes flickered in faint recognition; somewhere in the back of his drunken mind he had seen that look of fear before. It reminded him of a rabbit caught in the headlights of a car, wanting to run away but frozen by fear.

Suddenly as if someone had turned on a light within his brain, the penny dropped.

"Pearly, Pearly, come and give old Adie a kiss for old times' sake."

Malcolm was thrilled; the choirmaster had been lavish in his praise about the clarity and power of Malcolm's voice and he couldn't wait to tell Pearl. He was feeling a little guilty about leaving her to wander around London all on her own. If he had known his audition was going to be such a success he would have been only too pleased for her to have stayed.

Watching Pearl walking towards him, Malcolm could not help noticing that she seemed to have an air of self-confidence about her that he had not seen before. Perhaps this was the new independent Pearl that he knew was under the surface but had yet to emerge. Or was it the fact that she was wearing a brand new pair of stylish leather boots. Malcolm was only too well aware what a boost to the morale a woman got out of a shopping trip.

Pearl had enjoyed one of the best mornings of her life so far. At long last she had conquered her demons, and bought herself a new pair of boots into the bargain. Very soon now, some less fortunate soul would recover her old discarded ones from the roadside bin and two people would have had a successful morning. No longer would she be imprisoned by her past. And in part it was all due to Malcolm. It was because of him that they had travelled up to London in the first place. It was also on Malcolm's advice she had worn those boots.

Pearl could still hear the scream as her foot connected with Adrian Parker's genitals. Come to that so could everyone within half a mile of Oxford Street at the time. The feeling of satisfaction as the heavy leather buried itself deep into his groin would live with her for the rest of her life.

19

The Return Flight

Time on the return flight from Cork seemed to pass much quicker than the outward one. David barely had a chance to mull over the events of the weekend before it was time to fasten his seat belt for landing. The meeting with his natural mother had proved to be a traumatic event for them both and David's mind was full of conflicting emotions, not least the thought that he might in some way have been disloyal to the memory of his adoptive parents. The very fact that he kept thinking of his biological ancestry and what it might unfold filled him with a sense of guilt.

But at least now he knew the truth, or half of it anyway, and David felt sure that it wouldn't be long before he uncovered the whole story. Sarah Sheridan at 18 had found herself pregnant in a strange country. Thrown out of the family home by a distraught father she had eventually found her way into the surgery of Dr Samuel Cohen. Instead of condemning her for being in the condition that she found herself, he had shown her nothing but sympathy and kindness. He had, however, refused to assist her in terminating her pregnancy, and instead had invited her into his home until after the birth of her baby, on the excuse that she would be company for his wife Rebecca.

Sarah and Rebecca had formed an immediate bond, and on discovering that Rebecca was unable to have children of her own, Sarah offered to let her adopt the unborn child. As difficult as this decision had been for her, Sarah realised that to allow her baby to be brought up in a wealthy middle-class family was far better than him or her being raised in a poor single-parent one. David realised this to be true from his experience at the surgery; he also knew how devastating it was for young single girls to give up their babies for adoption. Even in this day and age, let alone how it would have been nearly 50 years ago.

So now at least David knew how he became the only child in a middle-class Jewish family. The one remaining mystery to be solved was the identity of his natural father. When he had first met Sarah, David strongly suspected that Samuel could be the one, but the sincere way Sarah explained the circumstances that had led her to allow him to be adopted dispelled that theory. Anyhow the fact that Rebecca had kept Sarah informed of her son's progress through life, in his opinion was further proof that Sarah had told the truth. His knowledge of women told him that no way would Rebecca have kept in such close contact with a woman that had had an affair with her husband, a woman that had provided him with the one thing that she was unable to, let alone allow her husband to leave that person a considerable amount of money in his will.

With these thoughts in mind David asked Sarah directly if she knew who his natural father was. The look of hurt in her eyes, however, made him wish he had held his tongue. Holding back the tears she explained to him that his father was, and would be, the only man she had ever loved. "Then why are you here, working as a housekeeper to a retired priest, he asked. Was my father a married man, and more importantly, is he still alive?"

Sarah remained silent for a moment deep in thought. David could see that she was struggling to contain her emotions. Eventually she plucked up the courage to look him in the eye. Her voice was soft but steady. "Your father is still alive,

David, and yes in a way I suppose you could say he was married, but not in a conventional way, and definitely not at the time that you were conceived. At that time he was free, but too young to bear the responsibility of a wife and baby; that and only that is the reason. I never told him of your existence until quite recently. As for my living here as housekeeper, as you put it, I have my reasons. I beg you not to press me on the matter. I do promise you, however, that when I have spoken to your father, and if he is in agreement, I will arrange for the two of you to meet."

Reluctantly David agreed to his mother's request; he really did not have much choice in the matter. The last thing he wanted was to cause any more pain or distress; there had been enough of that already. But it still didn't stop him from speculating.

Why Sarah had been so reluctant to talk about his father was beyond David. OK she had explained the circumstances under which she had found herself pregnant, and the fact that his father was at the time far too young and inexperienced to be saddled with a wife and baby, but after all these years surely he should step forward and take some of the responsibility for his actions, now that he knew of David's existence. But then David also knew from his experiences at the surgery that fathers could be an elusive breed when it came to discovering their whereabouts.

Martha would be pleased for him; he had already phoned to inform her of his success, and was pleased when she suggested he invited his newly found mother to their wedding in the spring. What David had not told her, however, was that he had already invited her to join him directly after Christmas. He had high hopes of Sarah persuading his father to come along with her. David also knew that Martha was wrapped up in the preparations for Tom Hall's centenary, so he thought it best not to tell her until he was sure that both his parents were coming. Sarah had hinted that if his biological father wanted to remain undiscovered she would be travelling to England alone.

*

Gatwick airport viewed from the air looked like a city in its own right, with its vast terminal buildings lit up like fairyland, and the runways with their multi-coloured lamps guiding the departing and incoming planes as they went about their business. David felt like a visiting alien from some distant planet, poised to invade the earth. The city of Gatwick was about to be engulfed by a superior race who would at last restrain this ever-growing menace, together with the countless others that had spread all over the world. For a brief moment David imagined he was the commander in chief of operations, ready to strike the first blow to free mankind from the ever-growing menace of rampant expansion. After years of eating up the English countryside like some uncontrollable disease, the time for retribution had arrived.

The bump as the wheels of the aircraft touched down jolted David back to reality. The make-believe city of Gatwick had resumed its role as an airport once again.

As David walked through the never-ending corridors to baggage reclaim, silent vehicles overtook him, ferrying the old and infirm backwards and forwards. Like creatures from another planet, they sat motionless awaiting their fate, lost and alone in the middle of an enormous metropolis. Oh how lucky he was to be able live in Eastbourne, with its old-fashioned shops and quaint little houses; it was like returning to an oasis in the middle of a vast desert.

David felt the vibration of his mobile phone. It was Martha, eager to learn the latest news about his parents. As he related the events of the past few days and heard Martha's excited response, David was suddenly aware of how lucky he was to have found love so late in life. He was determined that nothing on this earth would be allowed to spoil it for them. It took all of David's willpower not to blurt out that he had invited his mother to meet her in time for Tom's birthday celebrations; he wanted that to be a pleasant surprise.

20

Warning

Tom was feeling rather tired today, and that bloody indigestion wasn't helping things. Why everyone had to make such a pig of themselves over the Christmas period was beyond him. As far as he was concerned it was all an unnecessary fuss about nothing, just like his birthday tomorrow. He couldn't wait to get that all over and done with so that the home could get back to normal again.

Martha Branigan had set herself up as some sort of commander in chief of operations and woe betide anyone who crossed her at the moment. Not that Tom had any intention of doing so; the last thing he needed right now was an altercation with her. He decided that instead of worrying Martha he would ask Mary to bring him something for his indigestion, after all it was probably the stress and strain of everything that was going on at the moment that was causing it in the first place. If he asked Martha, or Pearl come to that, they would no doubt immediately insist on calling Doctor David Cohen, and he had got enough on his plate at the moment by all accounts. What with his forthcoming marriage to Martha early next year, and if the rumours going round about him finding out that he was an adopted child were true, the poor man had got Tom's sympathy. It was either a very brave or a very stupid man that took on Martha Branigan. But Tom knew from experience that loneliness could drive a person to do the most foolish things. Then there was the story circulating Sea View at the moment about Doctor David's newfound parents; if the rumours were correct, the guy needed all the help and understanding he could get. Both Pearl and Mary had informed Tom that David's parents had arrived from Ireland over Christmas and that his mother had turned out to be a 'lady of the night'. Even worse, his father was a priest! If the story were only half true, poor old Dr David's future seemed to be in for a stormy ride.

Tom sat back in his chair and mulled over the events that had help shape his own life. By far and away the best one was meeting Jenny. The worst was when she died. In between there had been many ups and downs, mostly ups. When the boys were born, first Graham and two years later Anthony, for instance. Tom was rather sad that they had never been blessed with a girl; it would be nice now that he was on his own to have had a daughter, someone to look out for him in his old age. Daughter-in-laws were OK, he had been blessed with two lovely daughters-in-law, but he imagined they could never be as close as a daughter.

He closed his eyes and tried to remember all the happy times he had had with Jenny. There were so many; if only he hadn't spoilt it all by having an affair. Fiona had been his only lapse during the whole time that he was married. In his younger days before he met Jenny there were a few dalliances with the ladies; they were hard to avoid if you worked in the building trade. But apart from Fiona Tom had stayed on the straight and narrow. As much as he tried to deny it to himself Tom knew that she had been something special. Even now, despite his age, and the recurrent guilt, the thought of her made his pulse race. Tom felt that if only he could have explained in some way to Jenny that it was possible for a man to love two women at the same time, life would have been less fraught. However, Tom knew that would have been impossible. No woman would accept that scenario, and he was doing himself no good by keep harping back into his past.

They were happening more often lately, these little flashbacks. Every time Tom thought of Jenny his thoughts would eventually revert back to the time he had nearly lost her. He was sure Jenny was looking down from above and reminding him of his lapse, just to punish him. Why else was he living so long? He was only human, and Fiona had been a fine looking woman. If only Jenny hadn't been going through one of her periods of depression. But there he was again, blaming her for something that was entirely his fault.

Bringing up two young children must have been very stressful and tiring; no wonder she was always too tired when they went to bed, and Tom knew he hadn't been much help. Working as many hours as he did, when starting up his own company. But it had been a good business; it turned out to be one of the best moves in his life. Even that he wouldn't have been able to do if it wasn't for Jenny. It was Jenny who went out to work until he got the business established. She was the one who still found time to do all his office work as well as keeping the home going. No wonder she was always tired, and he had repaid her by shagging the first attractive woman that made a pass at him.

A sharp rap on the door disturbed Tom's thoughts, and before he could call out to whoever it was to come in, the door burst open and in strode Martha Branigan, followed by a rather nervous looking Pearl.

"Good morning, Thomas, I trust you are feeling well today. Are you looking forward to tomorrow?" Martha did not wait for a reply. Determined that Tom should not interrupt her, she continued, "I have arranged a reception in the lounge, where I shall greet the members of the press, together with our local member of parliament as well as the Lord and Lady Mayor.

After presenting you with your customary congratulatory card from the King, I will make a speech thanking the guests for attending your birthday celebrations. I shall also then tell them how much you have enjoyed your time here with us, and how well you have been looked after. I have purchased a small gift on your behalf, which I thought you would like to present to me in front of the local dignitaries. If there are any members of your family present they can join you afterwards for tea in the lounge. I don't think that will put too much of a strain on you, Thomas. If you have any queries please have a word with Pearl. But I warn you, Thomas, if you think you can get up to your old tricks by pretending you are not feeling up to it, you can think again. I have put a lot of hard work and effort into planning these celebrations and nobody – and I mean nobody, is going to spoil my day." With that Martha turned, glared at Pearl and left the room.

Tom and Pearl looked at one another for a moment in silence, before Pearl exploded. "Her day!" she exclaimed. "Her day. Who does she think she is? I know one thing for sure, she certainly suffers from 'I' trouble; she said 'I' so many times I expected her to be wearing an eye patch and waving a cutlass about. Bloody cheek, and she's bought herself a fucking present. Oh I'm sorry, Tom, I didn't mean to swear, but she gets on my tits. Blimey, there I go again."

Tom laughed. There was something different about Pearl this morning that he could not quite put his finger on. Ever since she had returned from her trip to London yesterday, Pearl had somehow become more confident in herself, more relaxed. She certainly would not have spoken about Martha in such a manner a few weeks ago, not in front of him anyway. It was probably the influence of that young man she was going out with. "Don't worry about it, Pearl, I've heard worse; anyway Martha's enough to make a saint swear. She might think she has got one over on me at the moment but I'll find a way to get my own back on her, you mark my words my girl."

Pearl looked at Tom; he reminded her so much of her Grandpa; when he set his mind to do something there was no stopping him. The way he looked at her with those lovely dark eyes, the smile that could charm the birds from the trees. Little wonder that in his day Tom had proved to be such a success with ladies. Why, if he was 60 years younger she might even fall for him herself. But it was hard to imagine Martha not getting her own way this time; with less than 24 hours to go before the big event she had got the upper hand.

Martha sat at her desk sipping her coffee and biting on a cream doughnut. She felt quite pleased with herself; life at the moment was all going her way. David had found his mother, and his father, which came as quite a shock to the system when it was revealed that he was a priest. Who would have bet on David's father being a man of the cloth? And she, Martha Branigan, was about to advance her standing within the community by becoming the doctor's wife. If she could persuade her future father-in-law to officiate at the wedding, her happiness would be complete. But if he knew David intended to wear his yarmulke he would in all probability decline. Above all, she had just told Tom Hall in no uncertain terms what was going to happen tomorrow.

What a stubborn old bugger Tom could be when he wanted to! Well she had told him this time. If things went well tomorrow, and she saw no reason why they should not, Martha decided she would have another go at getting him to move in with one of the other residents. It was ridiculous that he should occupy the best room in the home all on his own. This time Martha intended to be more insistent, maybe on the grounds that Tom needed specialised care or that he was not capable of making up his own mind. On reflection she didn't think she would get away with that one; even David, who she could twist round her little finger, had said that for his age

Tom Hall still retained all his marbles. Sometimes Tom even made her feel quite vulnerable, when he looked at her with those dark brown eyes of his, eyes that seemed to peer right into her very soul; so much so that Martha was sure he knew her innermost thoughts. No, she would bide her time. It was no good getting herself all worked up, especially today of all days. She would leave it a bit longer; after all, there was only one more day to go.

21

Departure

Mary set the alarm clock at the side of her bed for 6 a.m. She was on duty tomorrow and wanted to be the first one to wish Tom a happy birthday. Everybody else on the staff, from Martha right down to the kitchen porter, would also be on duty and under strict instructions to make sure they were on time and well turned out for the occasion. Martha had been adamant about that. Tomorrow was a big day for the home, with all the local bigwigs and the national press in attendance; if anyone screwed up, their life wouldn't be worth living. Mary had got the message that Martha was determined to shine and woe betide anyone who thought otherwise. Well, she would not be the one to throw a spanner in the works. Mary may not have been at the home all that length of time, but had learned already that you did not cross Martha Branigan.

Anyway Mary liked Tom, and would do everything in her power to make his big day pass without incident. Sea View had been like a home from home to her since she had left the comfort of her parents' house and she had no intention of letting him or Sea View down at this late stage; especially when they were about to get some much needed publicity. Satisfied in her own mind that she was prepared for all eventualities, Mary made herself a hot drink before jumping into bed to settle down for the night with one of her favourite books.

In the next room, Pearl was deep in thought; she had just put the phone down after speaking to Malcolm and needed time to think. He had asked her to consider giving up her job at the home and move to London with him. He had been offered promotion within the company he worked for and was reluctant to pass up the opportunity. But apart from that there was more than an even chance of him joining the choir in Westminster Abbey. Their visit up to London the other day had all but confirmed that he would be accepted and Malcolm had been beside himself with excitement; so much so that Pearl hadn't had time to tell him about her escapade while wandering round the capital on her own.

There was also the problem still to be solved of introducing Malcolm to her mother. If she turned up with him one day and told her they were off to London the next week, Joyce would not be best pleased.

The sooner Pearl overcame this obstacle the better. Maybe she should come clean and admit to her mother that she had been seeing Malcolm for months.

Pearl would miss Sea View if she did decide to leave. Over the years that she had worked there she had made many friends, both within the home and outside. She would also miss the choir. It was doubtful if she were good enough to sing for Westminster Abbey, although Malcolm seemed to think otherwise. Time enough, however, to come to a decision about these matters after tomorrow when the dust had settled from Tom's centenary celebrations. By then she would have made up her mind one way or the other, depending, of course, on how Martha Branigan treated her during the festivities. If she got on her high horse too much Pearl would tell her in no uncertain terms where to stick her job. Pushing all these thoughts to the back of her mind, Pearl took a quick shower and prepared for bed.

Over at the main building Tom was not having a very good night. Whether or not it was the thought of all the fuss that was being created over his birthday tomorrow he didn't know. Or it might be the incident with Martha earlier in the day. He was too old and tired now to do battle with her; in his opinion the sooner he died and joined Jenny the better.

Earlier in the evening Martha had offered him a sedative to help him sleep. When he had declined, she had placed it, together with a glass of water, on the little cabinet by the side of his bed. "Just in case you change your mind, Thomas," she said, " I don't want you to be stressed out and unwell for tomorrow."

Tom sighed and reached over for the pill. Popping it in his mouth he downed it with the help of the water and lay back to try and get some sleep, but every time he closed his eyes he started to get strange images appearing in his mind, images from his past that he would rather not see.

Fighting to stay conscious, Tom regretted ever taking the sedative, but it was too late now. He could feel himself losing the battle to stay awake.

Tom could feel himself tumbling down a steep stone staircase. As he reached the bottom he found himself at the entrance to a long dark tunnel, and yet he was unhurt by his fall. Struggling to his feet Tom peered into the darkness; strangely familiar figures adorning the walls turned to stare at him as he entered. They were all his old friends from the past, pointing at him and calling him names. Adulterer. Fornicator. Liar. Cheat. How did they know, who had told them his innermost secrets? Tom could not understand why they all seemed to hate him so much. And all the time they were urging him on. It was as if he had a huge weight on his back and it was getting heavier every minute. As he passed each figure adorning the walls of the tunnel they disappeared, only to emerge again in a never-ending cycle. He started to run. The quicker he ran the faster they appeared, and all the time laughing at him. Exhausted, Tom paused to rest, covering his eyes to avoid looking at his tormentors, until eventually it grew silent.

Tom uncovered his face and looked around him. The figures had manifested into holographic images depicting his past. He could see himself walking along a strange highway holding a woman's hand. He looked up into her eyes; it was his mother. She was young and he was an old man. Tom covered his face to block out her image, but all that seemed to do was magnify the picture in his mind.

Calling out her name Tom tried to embrace her. He threw his arms around her but she melted away in his embrace. And still his tormentors were laughing at him.

At last Tom saw a friendly face. Robert was walking towards him, holding hands with a young man dressed in a yellow suit, a long cigarette holder held with an exaggerated air as he blew smoke rings into the air. Tom knew instantly that it was Simon, but how did he get hold of the cigarette holder? It was still on the table at the side of his bed. The couple smiled and waved at him as they strolled by, before vanishing in a puff of smoke.

Tom was sure Martha Branigan was leaning over him, wiping his fevered brow with the 'happy birthday' bunting used to decorate his room. Why was she grinning at him like some imbecile?

Suddenly Tom saw Jenny, his beloved Jenny; she was weeping uncontrollably, asking why? "Why Tom, why?" Her voice pierced deep into his brain. He begged her not to cry as he ran towards her pleading for forgiveness, only for her to evaporate before his eyes. Tom fell in a crumpled heap onto the stone floor; he wanted to just lie there and die. But no, he couldn't, he must find Jenny. In desperation he called out her name. The slender figure reappeared with her back towards him. Tom struggled to his feet. His burden was getting heavier and heavier but he forced himself on.

"Jenny, Jenny." The figure turned to smile at him. It was Fiona. Frantic now, Tom fought to awake from this nightmare. If only he hadn't taken that bloody sleeping pill. It was all Martha Branigan's fault. The more he tried to force himself back to consciousness, the further down the tunnel he seemed to fall.

Tom could feel somebody wiping his face. It was cool and soothing as he waited for the feeling of relief to change back into a nightmare, but it didn't. He could hear his name being called softly, over and over again. At last he recognised the voice. It was Mary, beautiful kind Mary. She had come to his rescue.

Mary woke with a start. She looked at her watch, it was a quarter to seven. Why hadn't the alarm gone off? Jumping out of bed she made a grab for her uniform, only for it to catch on the back of the chair. The sound of the buttons coming off the front of her dress and hitting the floor made her curse. Today of all days. Well, she couldn't stop and sew them back on again now; it would have to wait until she had been over to see Tom. Mary decided that for the moment she would have to rely on safety pins. She quickly dressed and after making emergency repairs to the gaping hole at the front of her uniform, made her way over to the main building.

As Mary passed Pearl's door she could hear someone moving about inside. Reassured that somebody would soon be following her, Mary made her way across to the main building and along the corridor to Tom's room. Knocking gently on his door she entered.

Tom was lying on his bed with his back towards her. His shoulders were heaving as though he was sobbing and he was sweating profusely. Filled with alarm Mary strode towards him. She knew it was a mistake after the second stride. The temporary fastening of her uniform parted as she reached the bedside, but it was too late now. Bending over, Mary mopped Tom's sweating brow with a handkerchief, softly calling out his name. "Tom, Tom, wake up; it's time to go now."

Tom turned over to greet his saviour. "Time to go where?" His mind was confused. Was that Mary talking to him, or was he still embroiled in his nightmare? And then Tom saw it; there it was not six inches from his face. The indigestion from the day before returned with a vengeance. It was as if his chest was being crushed in a vice. He gasped for air but the pain increased. His eyes bulged as he gasped for breath. Right there in front of him, high up on Mary's inner thigh was the birthmark, the elongated chevron. Jenny's tick of approval.

Mary's screams brought Pearl running, closely followed by a breathless Martha. As they entered the room Mary was on her knees cradling Tom's head in her arms. Martha was by now standing in the doorway, rooted to the spot as Pearl took control. She walked over to where Tom lay in Mary's arms and quickly felt for a pulse; there wasn't one.

Realising that it was too late Pearl gently closed Tom's staring eyes with her thumb and forefinger before turning to Martha and announcing, "I am afraid Tom is dead, Martha, there is nothing we can do here now, I suggest you phone Dr David Cohen."

Martha stood there stunned. All her months of preparation had been for nothing. Today was supposed to be the culmination of all her hard work; the press was arriving as Pearl spoke. The member of parliament and the other dignitaries were probably on their way right now. What would she say to them? "I'm sorry folks, Tom Hall is dead, go home." Suddenly anger took over from her shock. "You bastard, Tom Hall, you bastard!" she screamed. "Of all the days to die you had to choose today; what have I done to you to deserve this? There was only one more day to go. Then you could have died any time you wanted. With that outburst Martha collapsed in a heap on the floor and sobbed. Mary and Pearl stood silently by, heads bowed out of respect for Tom. Born 28.12.1938, died 28.12.2038 he had not only achieved his goal, he had got one over on Martha Branigan.

The deep rich voice echoed around the Lady Chapel as Malcolm brought the singing to a close. All Things Bright and Beautiful seemed an apt choice of hymn under the circumstances.

Despite the fact that the small gathering was attending a funeral, the general atmosphere was one of celebration rather than of mourning.

As if prompted by the cue master in a vast theatre, the clouds parted, allowing the star of the show to take a bow. The delicate rays of the winter sun peeked through the stained glass window onto the coffin where Tom lay. To the right of the altar, in the main body of the church, you could just see the flickering of candles in the Lady Chapel, placed there in memory of the recently departed by their loved ones. The mourners resumed their seats as the last strains of the music died away. For a few brief moments, each and every one of them reflected on how the occupant of the sarcophagus had touched their lives.

Anthony and Graham, together with their respective wives, sat at the front of the church in the pews that were reserved for members of the family. Each wrapped up in their own private memories of bygone days. Days when Tom played football with them in the park or of the times when he would challenge them to a race across the playing field opposite the house, and beat them every time. Throughout the whole of their lives he had always been there for them, no matter what. They suspected that during his lifetime their father had had many demons to come to terms with, but as usual he had confronted them in his own way. Now he was no more and they prayed that he was at peace with their mother.

The grandchildren and great grandchildren, seated in the pews behind, had flown in from all over the world, some of whom had never met Tom. They were there chiefly to pay their respects to a man whose reputation in the family was legendary. And also, with a bit of luck, may have mentioned them in his will. Mainly, however, they were in attendance because Anthony and Graham had instructed them to be there.

Father William O'Connor rose from his seat and approached the podium. He had never even met Tom Hall, let alone present a eulogy on his behalf. But in the absence of anyone else, owing to Tom's lack of religious conviction, he had been asked to do so. David and Martha had requested this of him, so how could he refuse? Time enough, perhaps, to shatter their dreams when this sad affair was over.

Pearl sat between Malcolm and Mary with her head bowed as Father William began his address. Her eyes strayed towards the coffin; she couldn't help thinking that this was the end of an era. It had disturbed her greatly that in death Tom had seemed so terrified; he had been such a lovely man, never failing to surprise her with his knowledge and understanding of life. The body may have worn out, but his mind had been active and enquiring right to the end, despite his age.

Mary nudged Pearl gently and pointed towards the floral tributes. There was an arrangement with a card attached, stating that it was from all the residents and staff of Sea View nursing home, and another small but pretty bouquet with the simple message 'As promised' from Mary and Pearl. But what had caught Mary's eye was the single red rose that had been placed discreetly at the foot of the coffin. It hadn't been there late last night, when Mary had popped in to say a prayer for Tom. Pearl turned to look at Mary and smiled; even in death the old rogue still surprised them. What would she give to know the secrets of his past.

A movement behind them made the two girls glance round. A woman in her 60s had entered the main body of the church and was standing silently, listening, head bowed as if in prayer. Unable to contain their curiosity Mary and Pearl's eyes followed her as she quietly moved along the narrow isle between the pews making her way to the Lady Chapel. Reaching the array of flickering flames, Samantha lit a candle and placed it by the side of the altar, before leaving through a side door.

Samantha Edwards stepped out into the fresh air and let out a sigh of relief. It had been a long and stressful few months. When she had finally decided to get rid of all her late mother's belongings, little did she realise what an effect it would have on her. Those old letters, written but never posted, must have lain there for years, locked away in her old tin box. If her grandson hadn't have asked her if she had anything he could keep his treasures in, they would still be there now.

Happily married for nearly 40 years before losing her beloved Jim last year, Samantha wished he were still around for her to share her troubles with. The children were not much help in these matters. Grown up with families of their own, they had little time to listen to her problems. Samantha knew that if she did unburden her worries to them, they would think it was all a huge joke. Jim had been right all along; she was too slow to catch a cold. If only she had been brave enough to visit Tom after discovering his whereabouts months ago.

Lengthening her stride, Samantha decided that it was best to let the past stay in the past where it belonged. She took a deep breath. Yes, bygones are bygones. Both Tom and her mother should be allowed to rest in peace, but she couldn't help thinking what might have been. "Fiona Philips," said Samantha out loud, "one day you will have a lot of explaining to do."